Subliminal

Tuanika

Editing: 21st Street Urban Editing & Publishing

ISBN: 978-0-692-3100-07
LCCN: 1-1858230371

Acknowledgements

I dedicate this to my kids for being the driving force in my life to strive for greatness. My family for loving me even when I didn't love myself and always sticking by me. Also, my friends for dealing with my craziness while loving my flaws and for being loyal. I couldn't be a better me without your love and support.

Chapter 1
Where It All Started

I'm laying here staring at the time displayed in blue lights on my ceiling. The alarm clock is blasting the Hot 97 Morning Show, and I'm thinking about how I let the salesman at P.C. Richards talk me in to buying this shit. My boyfriend, Ty, hates it. Right on cue, he wakes up, throws the pillow at me, and says, "Oh my God, turn that shit off." My body wants just five more minutes, but my mind is telling me to get up, because I know I have a busy day. I drag myself out the bed and hit the bathroom.

I love music so much that it's everywhere I am. I remember when I was younger, I used to take my radio from my room and put it in the bathroom and kitchen, so I could have music on while cooking, cleaning, and showering. Now that I'm grown and successful, the first major adjustment I made to the condo Ty and I purchased was having a top-of-the-line entertainment system and surround sound installed in every room. Now all I have to do is press a button and I have music everywhere; it's like heaven.

Ty's first upgrade to the condo was heating the floor in the bathroom. Like me, Ty grew up in a lower-class, single-parent household. His mother worked her ass off to make sure he and his sister had what they needed. However, luxury items weren't an option. So now that he is successful, he also gets things that he never had a chance to have before. At first, I wondered why we needed heated floors; that's such a waste of money. But now it's mid-December in New Jersey at six in the morning. I greatly appreciate the heated floors and praise the person who invented them.

I brushed my teeth, washed my face, turned the music up, and stepped in the steaming hot shower. The hot water blended perfectly with the music, and I drifted off to a serene, melodic place as I lathered up with Pure Rain Lever 2000. I was snapped back into reality halfway thru my shower by the sound of the toilet seat lid hitting the back of the toilet and Ty peeing. I hate it when he does that, but I'm so used to it that I just roll my eyes and continue my shower. He opened the shower door and was watching me wash up while he brushed his teeth. At first, I acted unfazed and kept washing up, but when he took two fingers and started at my neck and slowly worked his way down my back, I was instantly turned on.

So I lathered up the washcloth, making it extra wet and soapy. I turned around and squeezed it, so the soapy water trickled down my breasts, stomach, and thighs.

Then, I started playing with myself, squeezing my breasts together, smiling at him, moaning, and playing with my juice box. The look in his eyes let me know what was on his mind.

"Lookin' for problems this morning, huh?" I asked him.

"Lookin' for you to start my day off right," Ty responded.

I turned around and let the suds run down my back and the crack of my ass. He threw the toothbrush in the sink, took his boxers off, hopped in the shower, and started kissing all over me. The water was so hot that the whole bathroom became steamy like a sauna.

Spontaneous sex is always the best. We turned the shower into a porn scene. The sex was so good that I didn't even care that my hair was getting messed up after I had just spent hours at the shop the day before getting it done. The steamy hot water was raining down on us. I brought the thunder, he brought the lightning, and together, we were the perfect storm. He lifted me up and put my back against the cold shower wall. As he slid his love inside of me, I wrapped my legs around his waist, locked my fingers behind his neck, and slowly and erotically grinded up and down on him.

I was dripping wet and it wasn't from the shower. He kissed his way down my neck and dug his teeth in, not hard enough to break the skin, but with enough passion to hurt and feel good at the same time.

"Shit!"

I was his and he knew it.

He traced my neck with his tongue, digging his teeth in again, a little harder this time. He palmed my ass with both hands, lifting me up and down all while sliding in and out of me with long, deep strokes. He kept squeezing harder, thrusting in and out faster and faster until he felt my legs shaking.

Then, he put me down, pushed me up against the wall, and kissed me while massaging my clit with two fingers. He passionately sucked my nipples, tickling them with his tongue. I pushed his head lower. Ty kissed his way down my stomach while I pushed his head lower. Then, he lifted my right leg up onto his shoulder. I leaned my head back against the wall, lost in the moment, as his thick, wet tongue slid in and out of me.

"Yes, right there. Don't stop, babe. I'm 'bout to come."

I panted as he sucked and nibbled until my juices flowed. Then, he slurped and swallowed like a pro. Just when I thought it was over, he stood up, kissed me, and turned me around, allowing me to taste my sweet nectar on his lips.

I put my hands on the wall, arched my back, and poked my ass out for him. He loved it when I poked my ass out, and just as I thought it, he smacked my ass and said, "Yeah baby, poke it out for me." He grabbed the back of my neck and drove his love inside of me. He started slow, grinding to the rhythm of my body, but I had been with Ty for several years, so I knew what turned him on, what turned him off, and what drove him crazy. Since he started my day off right, I wanted to leave him with something to think about at work, so I decided to drive him crazy.

I started pushing back, making my ass bounce off him while looking back at him and biting my bottom lip. He grabbed my hair, wrapped it around his hand, and pulled it while pounding me with heavy thrusts. I felt him reaching deeper inside me and knew he couldn't hold it much more.

"Give it to me. Throw that shit back, baby. I'm 'bout to come."

I felt him throbbing inside of me, and just when he was almost there, I pushed him back off me, got down on my knees in front of him, and let my soft wet lips pull his love juice out of him. I gave him a kiss and rested my head on his chest. We hugged for a minute, letting the water roll freely down our bodies. We finally washed up and got out, and I felt relaxed and exhausted. All I wanted to do was curl up in the bed like a baby and take a nap, but I was already running late, so I had to rush to get dressed in order to head to work.

Things between Ty and I are good now, but it wasn't always smooth sailing. We've been together for eight years now. When we met, I was eighteen and he was nineteen. We were both fresh out of high school. Ty was on his way to Delaware State College to pursue a career in business management. His first love was football; it was the reason he got a scholarship to go there. He was so sexy and charming. Girls were naturally drawn to him.

They would see us together and make comments, blatantly flirting with him right in front of me. That always triggered an argument, and then our time together would never continue as planned. He would always say, "Man, I ain't beat for these girls that fuck with everybody. They're just hatin' because they ain't got a good man. Guys they fuck with don't wanna be seen with them in public."

Deep down I knew it wasn't true, but when we were together, Ty had a way of making nothing else matter. While Ty was working his magic on and off the field, I was working on my bachelor's degree in criminal justice at Montclair State University. I always wanted to be a lawyer. Something about the thrill of proving someone's innocence in one of the most intimidating settings in this world got me going.

My mother, however, had other plans for me. She encourages my education and doesn't deter me from my dreams of being a lawyer, but she'd much rather I follow her footsteps and make a name for myself in the real estate world.

She's a successful real estate broker and wants to turn her office into a mother-daughter chain and go national like other big agencies. I can see the potential in her idea, even the opportunity to make a lot of money, but real estate just isn't my passion. So to keep her happy, as well as myself, I work at her office as an agent Saturday, Sunday, and Monday. I go to school Tuesday through Friday. I still live at home. My mom pays for me to go to school, because she's proud that I'm being positive and furthering my education. The money I make from real estate, I use to shop and live.

****

My early childhood wasn't as easy and comfortable as my life is now. Things didn't start going good for us until I was about sixteen. That's when my mom started becoming successful in real estate. My father wasn't a part of my life until I was eighteen due to his lifestyle and drug habit. When he and my mother met and fell in love, my dad was a tall, light-skinned, good looking young man with lots of friends and money. He and his friends were known for fast cars and getting fast money. My mom, on the contrary, came from a family of four that struggled to pay rent and buy food. This is why she was instantly drawn to his lifestyle.

He loved the fact that she was so innocent, naïve, and loyal. There was so much she'd never seen, done, or even knew about. He felt like she was the purest thing he'd ever had in his life, so he made her his girl. That's when everything changed. They fell madly in love. He treated her great, but he was damaging her life at the same time. My father and his friends sold drugs to support their lifestyles, and even though he kept my mother away from that part of his life as much as possible, one day something happened that changed both of their lives forever.

My mother was a virgin when she got with him, but that changed almost instantly. By the time my grandmother found out they were having sex, my mother was already two months pregnant with me. She didn't know the importance of safe sex, because my grandmother wasn't the type to sit down and talk about that. They didn't have a close bond or an emotionally open, mother-daughter relationship. The only emotion she expressed often was anger. This was due to the self-hatred she had over how her life turned out.

When my grandmother found out, she instantly kicked her out, because she hated my father. She told my mother, "If you want to ruin your life, you can do it somewhere else, 'cause this ain't how I raised you."

So just like that, my mom and my dad were officially on their own, which meant they needed more money to live. This meant my dad needed to sell more drugs.

One night, he and my mother were on their way to McDonald's to feed one of my mom's cravings. That's when my dad got a call for a large transaction from one of his customers. He figured he could kill two birds with one stone and be home for the night. He told my mom, "Lock the doors and wait here. I'm gonna go handle something with Dave. I'll be right back." She did as he said and locked the doors. When he got out, she leaned back in her seat, rubbing her stomach. She looked around nervously.

Dave met him outside of the rundown apartment building on the one-way side street, and they walked across the street and in through the backdoor of an apartment. Shortly after, my mom heard screaming and gunshots. She saw my dad come running full-speed towards the car. She unlocked the door, he jumped in the car, and he peeled off as fast possible. My Dad was crying and screaming, "He killed him! He killed him! Then, I had to kill him!" My mom was terrified and started crying as he sped home blowing through every stop sign. She fretted for her life the entire way home. When they got back to their apartment, my mom cried out in confusion, asking many questions, while my dad was drinking, crying, and pacing. When he finally calmed down a little bit, he told her what happened.

"When we got inside, the guy pulled a gun on us and tried to rob us. Dave refused to give up the drugs, and the guy shot him once in the head and once in the chest. I blacked out. Before I knew it, I grabbed the gun and we were tussling. I bit his face and locked on it like a pit bull. He then let the gun go and fell against the wall, holding his face. That's when I shot him twice in the chest."

My mom sunk her face in her hands and started crying uncontrollably.

"Why, why?" she cried. What are we gonna do now?"

He put the bottle of Jack Daniels down that he was drinking, sat down next to my mom, pulled her close, hugged her, and rocked her back and forth, trying to calm her down. "I don't know, baby. I don't know."

A couple days later, the cops came to the apartment and arrested my father. My mom tried to go back home, but my grandmother wasn't the forgiving type. She told my mom she wasn't welcome there. My grandmother reminded her how she had wrecked her life, going against everything she was taught. My mom was on her own, and my grandmother abruptly slammed the door in her face. My mom pregnant, devastated, and desperate, went to social services and got placed in a program.

They placed her in a women's home, Liberty Place, which was a program for single women with kids who had nothing and nowhere to go. She had me on May 10, and my father was already in jail waiting to be sentenced. Later on, she got a job and her own place. Ever since, it has been just us two. My father was sentenced to twenty years in prison and never saw me until later in my life, when I was about eighteen years old.

My mother struggled for most of my life working one dead-end job after another just to feed me and pay the bills. Then, one day while packaging pills at a warehouse, she overheard one of the girls she worked with talking about a real estate job she was about to start and how this was her last week at the warehouse. My mom jumped in the conversation asking questions and mentally taking notes, because she was determined to move up in the world and make a better life for us. She ended up taking the course, passing the test, and getting a job as a real estate agent.

After her first couple of commissions, things started getting a little better for us. It wasn't steady money, but it produced lump sums of money at a time, and she learned how to budget her money and make things work. After a couple years in, she got better and better and so did our lifestyle. While our lives were finally getting on track, my father's was getting worse. After he was released, he quickly realized how different the world was and had a hard time adjusting and finding work to make money.

He contacted my mom asking to see me, so she let him come by. I had never seen my father throughout his entire sentence in prison, nor did I receive any letters or phone calls from him. As far as I know, my mother never paid him a visit or spoke with him. She said she had written him a few times over the years, but just couldn't deal with what he was going through, because she had too much to deal with out here in the real world.

I didn't know what to expect when I met him. I knew the story of their past together, but I also knew he was never a part of my life. I didn't know him and I wasn't sure if he really wanted to see me or if this was just his way back to the most stable thing he'd ever had in his life: my mom. The day finally came and it was very awkward. The doorbell rang. My mom opened the door; it was him. They just stood there for a minute staring at each other, and then he reached out for a hug. She hugged him and took a step back.

"Wow, it's been a long time. I'm glad to see you're healthy and free."

"It hasn't been easy, but I've managed. I thought about you and baby girl almost every day. How is she?"

"She's good, all grown up now, doing good in college and working with me at the office. You missed a lot, but hopefully you can get to know each other and make up for lost time."

"I would love that," he replied with a smile.

"Well, come in and shut the door. I'll get her for you." She walked to the bottom of the stairs and shouted, "Tammy, come down here. There's someone here to see you." He stood in the foyer watching me walk down the stairs with the smile of a proud parent on his face.

I don't know what I expected to feel, but I felt nothing. I noticed a slight resemblance, but I felt no connection.

"Hey, baby girl." He bear hugged me, lifting me off of the ground.

"Wow, look at you, just as beautiful as your mother." "Thanks," was all I could muster up to say to him.

"I'm sorry I haven't been here for you, but that's over now, baby girl. I'm gonna get my life right and make sure I'm a part of yours every step of the way."

He kept calling me baby girl and all I kept thinking was, I ain't no baby; you missed that part. I guess I harbored some resentment toward him because of how hard my mom and I had it. Now when we're finally doing good, he wants to pop up and be part of the picture. I think my mom felt it too, because she wasn't all warm and mushy with him. She wasn't nasty to him either. She just kept things real short with him.

After my father's visit and a couple more, I started to notice a change in him. Then, the visits stopped. One night, I heard my mom talking to her friend, Gwen, on the phone in her room. She was telling her how she can't believe after all this time away he came home and got worse. Instead of selling drugs, he started using them. When I heard that, I had to walk away. I went in my room, layed down on my bed, and let the news sink in. My father was a hustler and a killer. He was locked up for almost twenty years, and now he's getting high.

It hurt when I said it to myself, and then I thought about my mom. If it hurt me, it must be killing her. From that point on, my mom cut him off and went right back to how things were when he was locked up. This all went down a couple of years ago. Since then, things have gotten better for us and my father is back in jail. This time, for armed robbery. Sometimes I wonder what part of him I inherited—the good part or the crazy part.

☐

Chapter 2
Growth

Everybody out here had a circle of friends they ran with. I kept my circle tight, because I'd learned the hard way in high school the drama having too many friends from different cliques can bring. Through all the bullshit, my friends, Mia and Kasey, remained the same. They were loyal to me, and we went through a lot of shit together. Now, we're like family. Mia and I have lived in the same neighborhood since sixth grade. She lived four doors down from me. We truly grew up and learned everything together.

Her cousin, Kasey, was from Elizabeth. She used to stay at Mia's a lot, because their mothers were sisters and Kasey's mom worked a lot. After a while, Kasey's mom got a job in Atlanta and Kasey didn't want to go, so Mia's mom said she could stay with them. From that point on, we were all inseparable.

We went through all our phases in fashion together. From TLC to Destiny's Child, we were on every new style that came out. Mary J. Blige was my idol. Her songs were like our anthems. We learned how to drive together, got drunk together, and started messing with boys around the same time. I wish things were still like that now.

Fashion played a big part in our lives. How you dress, what you drive, and who your clique is speaks for who you are. We were raised in that era. We came from lower-class families, which is why we experienced so much. There were good parts and hood parts in the area where we lived. I picked up a lot of knowledge from both. My mother always told me that struggle makes you stronger; she was definitely right. There was always something going on in our area, both day and night.

They say New York is the city that never sleeps. Well, my city must be related, because it doesn't rest either. I was trying to get some good sleep, so I could be fresh and well rested for the party Mia, Kasey, and I were going to that night, but that was easier said than done. I was awakened by the sound of a woman screaming, "Call the cops; he's gonna kill me!"

Those are my neighbors. They live directly next to us on the left. This was like a routine for them. I would think something was wrong if they weren't fighting. In the beginning, when they first moved in, people were concerned and would call the cops to get involved. Her family even came a couple times and took her with them, but she would always come back. So now, nobody gets involved. One of these days, he's probably going to kill her. It won't be a shock to anyone. I've gotten so accustomed to it that most of the time I sleep through it, but this time was different.

I could hear him cursing at her and pausing in between each word to hit her. It was kind of like my mother did when we were bad and she beat us with the belt. They were so loud I couldn't sleep, so I just got up to shower. As usual, Ty slept through all the commotion. He's such a heavy sleeper and can sleep through anything. He didn't even feel me get out the bed. I did my usual routine, turned on the music in the bathroom, and hopped in the steaming hot shower.

I got out, got dressed, and woke Ty up by kissing him on the cheek.

"Babe, I'm out. Me and Mia are going shopping. I'll be back in a little bit."

As I stood up, he opened his eyes, grabbed me, and pulled me back toward the bed.

"Come here. Why you leaving me?" He was kissing on my neck and unbuttoned my jeans. I knew where it was going. I was definitely with it, but in the back of my mind, I knew Mia was waiting on me. He took my hand, put it in his boxers, and slid it up and down on his meat. It was ballgame after that. Mia had to wait.

While Ty and I were handling business, my phone kept going off. I knew it was Mia by the Nicki Minaj ringtone I had saved under her name. Every time I went to grab the phone, he would grab my hands, pin them down to the mattress, and thrust harder inside me. Ty had me so spellbound, by the third time she called, I was about to come. He felt it and started pounding me extra hard and we both came. I rolled over, put my head on his sweaty chest, and fell asleep.

I woke up to Nicki Minaj blaring from my phone, and I jumped up in a panic.

"Oh shit, what time is it?" I franticly asked Ty. "Mmmm, I don't know. Come on, babe; go back to sleep," he replied.

"No, I gotta get up. I gotta go meet Mia."

"Okay, bring me some Jordan's back." I gave him a kiss and ran in the bathroom to take another quick shower.

While I was getting dressed, I called Mia. "Hey girl, I'm so sorry. I'm on my way."

"Damn, I called you like ten times. Where are you?"

"I'm leaving my house right now. I'll be right there."

When I got there, she was already outside sitting in her boyfriend Keys' car talking on the phone.

I got out and immediately apologized, "I'm sorry, girl. You know how Ty is in the morning. I got caught up and lost track of time."

"Yeah, Yeah, Yeah... Here you go with the bullshit. You ready? We're taking Keys' car, because he has mine."

"Yeah Mia, I'm ready. Let's go." I tossed my bag in the backseat, shut the door, and we were off.

Keys has been Mia's on-and-off boyfriend for the past three years. His real name is Keyshawn, but they call him Keys because of what he sells. He was a caramel-colored pretty boy with hella swag. He hustled hard. Mia couldn't ask for much more. She silently prayed that his sex game was as good as his hustling skills. She would later find out it was. He had a pregnant girlfriend he lived with when they met. But outside of home, let him tell it, he was single as a dollar bill.

Things between Keys and Mia started off pretty normal. They would talk and flirt occasionally, but I saw where it was going. I warned Mia not to do it because it was a bad situation, but she just couldn't leave him alone. Before I knew it, they were sneaking off and fucking around. Of course his girlfriend had the baby and found out about them. Things then got ugly between her and Mia. They had several verbal and physical altercations, because Keys continued to openly have relationships with both of them. He would deny the other relationship whenever questioned by each female.

The back-and-forth game continued until one night the baby was sick and in the hospital. Keys' baby mama was looking for him and calling him non-stop. She couldn't find him and he wouldn't answer any of her calls. She knew he was with Mia, but she didn't have time to be chasing him around. She had the baby to worry about. So, she sent her sister to Mia's house to see if his car was out there. It wasn't right in front of Mia's house, but it was parked across the street, about two doors down from Mia's house.

I guess he thought no one would put two and two together, but they did. Her mother and sister came to the hospital a little later that night to give her a break, allowing her to go home to shower and eat. As soon as she left the hospital, she went straight to Mia's house. She stood next to Keys car with a tire iron in her hand and called his cell phone.

It went straight to voicemail once again. She waited for the beep then left him a message.

"Now it's over, bitch!"

She hung up and preceded to bust out all the windows in his car one by one. She also busted out the headlights.

Mia and Keys were in the middle of a hot and heavy sex session when he heard the car alarm going off and the sound of glass shattering and hitting the ground. He jumped up, ran to the window, and saw her tearing his car up. "That crazy ass bitch! I'm gonna kill her," he yelled as he rushed to put his clothes on and ran down the steps. Mia was putting her clothes on and took off running behind him.

He sprinted off the porch, hopped over all the stairs, and ran straight towards her. She was now busting out the windshield of Mia's car. "And that bitch gonna get it, too. I told you to stop playing with me," she screamed.

He grabbed her and they started fighting over the tire iron. The cops came flying down the street just in time to break everything up.

They took statements from Mia and the neighbors. They arrested Keys and his baby mama. Of course Mia bailed him out. He told her he'd get both of their cars fixed, then explained to her that he was going to give his baby mama's sister the money to bail her out, because the baby is in the hospital and needed her. He bailed her out, and then he stopped dealing with her unless it had to do directly with their son. I never approved of Mia and Keys' situation from day one, but that's my girl, so I ride with her no matter what. My mother always said, "The heart wants what the heart wants." If that's who she wanted, I had to accept it and respect it, even if I didn't like it.

We never shopped locally, because that's where all the girls around here shop. It's nothing worse than getting fly for an event and seeing a lame chick rocking the same outfit the wrong way. So we normally hit Philly, Elizabeth, or go up top to New York because they have way more variety. Plus, you can talk them down sometimes, especially if you're spending money. Between the two of us, we usually come out with good deals.

Today we decided to run through Philly to get a couple things. We bought some outfits, several pairs of shoes, and some accessories. Then we headed home.

We stopped at the corner store a few blocks from Mia's house and a car full of girls pulled up next to us. They blew their horn, motioning for us to put the window down.

Keys drove a black Audi A8 that sat on black twenty-two-inch rims with black tint. They couldn't see who was in it, but judging from the look on their faces when we rolled the windows down, I think it's safe to say they weren't expecting it to be us. Mia raised her shades up above her eyes and sarcastically asked, "Can I help you?" The driver looked confused. I could see the thoughts running through her head as she searched for a quick response.

Clearly they were looking for Keys, but Mia had a rep for being a hot head and a thoroughbred, so the girl knew not to come at her crazy. It was the longest ten second pause in the history of conversations.

She finally responded with "No sweetheart, I thought you were somebody else. My bad."

Mia pulled off, rolled the window up, looked at me, and started laughing. "I'm about to start taking his car more often and see what else I catch." We both laughed as she got out the car and went in the store. She got her usual turkey burger with everything, no tomato, and fries. Then she came back out to the car.

Ty called me while we were on our way back to Mia's house and asked me to meet him at my house, so I could take him to pick up his bike. The guy from the shop called and said it was ready. So we went back to Mia's, I grabbed my bags out the trunk, and put them in my car. "Okay girly, I'll call you in a little bit. I'm about to take Ty to pick up his bike."

"Okay, I'm gonna take the dog to Keys' house, because I'm staying there tonight after we come back from the party. Hit me when you're done getting dressed, so I know what time we're leaving."

"You got it, chica. Talk to you later," Mia said. I got into my car and pulled off.

****

I left and met Ty at our place and took him to pick up his bike from Stumpy's. He went riding with his boys, and I was on my way back home when I got a call from Kasey. "Hey Kase, wassup?"

"Tammy! Tammy! Oh my God! Somebody shot Mia!" she cried. I almost crashed when I heard those words. I pulled over so fast, I ran up on the curb. I straightened the car out, put it in park, and threw the shades on my face onto the floor.

Kase, stop playing, 'cause I'm not laughing. What are you talking about? I just left Mia like an hour ago and she was gonna take the dog to Keys' house."

"I don't know, Tammy. My friend called me and said there's a lot of cops and people over there at her house and that they took Mia away in ambulance, because she'd been shot!"

"Where? What happened?" I started crying. The tears started streaming uncontrollably down my face.

"Where is she?"

"They rushed her to the hospital. Meet me there, Tammy. Hurry up! I'm leaving now."

"I'm on my way," I said, and then hung up the phone. I instantly peeled off. I was driving fast and crying so hard, I didn't see or hear anything around me, not even the music in the car. This felt surreal, like I was having an outer-body experience.

Chapter 3
Shit Just Got Real

I got to the hospital and went straight to the nurses' station. I was crying so hard and was so out of breath from running, my heart was racing. I was drenched in sweat. They thought I was hurt and needed to be treated.

I caught my breath enough to muster, "I'm fine. My best friend Mia, where is she? Mia Walker! She's been shot."

The nurse told me to calm down and she tried to sit me down, but I couldn't sit or calm down. It felt like my heart was beating through my chest. I could hear it in my head. My thoughts were racing a million miles per minute through my brain. As she looked in the computer for Mia's name and status, my eyes were canvassing the ER waiting area for a familiar face.

I didn't see anybody I knew or that knew Mia. Then, the nurse came from behind the desk and gently grabbed me by my arm.

"Sweetie, she's in the trauma bay, but I can't let you back there without a family member." I could tell by the look on her face that there was something she wasn't telling me. I felt my blood boiling. I felt like knocking her the fuck out and just running back there, but I knew security would be all over me.

I looked at her with tears in my eyes and said, "Ma'am I understand your position, but that's like my sister; her family will tell you the same. Please let me back there. She's dying and I have to get back there." As I said those words, more tears started pouring down my face. Before she could respond, Kasey came running in crying. She saw me and the nurse and ran over to us.

"Where is she, Tammy? Where's Mia? Where's Mama Walker?"

"In the back. They won't let me in because I'm not immediate family."

Kasey looked at the nurse and said, "That's my cousin back there. Go get her mother; she'll tell you. You have to let us back there."

"Sweetheart, I can't let y'all back there. Only her parents are allowed back there right now.

I can't really tell you what's going on due to laws and regulations, but I'll let her mother know you're here. I understand that's your family and you are concerned, but I can't let you back there right now." Kasey started going crazy when she heard that.

"That's my fucking cousin! She's dying back there," she screamed at the nurse.

Then, she tried to push past me and the nurse to get back there. I grabbed her and the nurse started yelling for security. Kasey was crying, screaming, and altogether losing it. I was a mess inside, but I was trying to hold it together. I was trying to calm her down and get the nurse to relax so we weren't thrown out by security.

I took Kasey outside, so she could smoke a Newport, calm down a little, and call Mama Walker to let us in. She kept calling, but her phone kept going straight to voicemail. I could feel it. I could feel it in my gut and deep down in my soul. She was gone, but they just didn't want to tell us. Kasey chain-smoked cigarette after cigarette, and I paced back and forth in front of the emergency room entrance. Finally, we saw her aunt and some of her cousins pull up.

They got out of the car crying and came straight to us. Her aunt grabbed us and hugged us as tight as she could. Right then and there, my deepest fear was confirmed. My best friend was dead. Keys heard what happened and was calling my phone non-stop. When I answered, I was crying so hard I couldn't even talk.

He kept screaming in the phone, "Tammy, where is she? Where's Mia?"

All I could say is, "She's dead, Keys." Then I hung up the phone. I couldn't deal with him right now. I couldn't even deal with myself.

I couldn't figure it out. I was replaying our day in my mind trying to figure out what happened. Where did everything go wrong? Every time I tried to gather my thoughts, I couldn't get past my emotions enough to think clearly. All I could do is cry and try to make myself understand that I'll never see my best friend again. Mama Walker came out wiping her face, trying to pull herself together as she walked towards us. I couldn't even look her in the face. I knew I would completely lose it. Her sister, Mia's other aunt, ran up to her and hugged her. They both broke down in tears.

We all circled around hugging her, trying to give her strength and support. No matter how hard I tried, I couldn't make the tears stop. Keys showed up and went straight to Mama Walker and started hugging her crying and saying, "I'm so sorry. I'm so sorry. I'm gonna find out who did this, Mama." I couldn't take it anymore. I had to leave. I needed to be by myself. I went down to the beach and just sat there on a bench crying and thinking. I left my phone in the car, because I had my mom, Ty, Kasey, Keys, and half the town calling.

News traveled fast where we lived. I was the closest person to Mia besides Keys, so everybody had questions and comments for me. I didn't want to hear anything but my best friend's voice. I couldn't quite wrap my mind around the fact that I would never hear it again. I stayed at the beach until the sun went down, and then I headed to my mom's house.

I returned Ty's calls on my way there. He was going crazy.

"Oh my God! Where are you? Everybody's going crazy looking for you. We thought something happened to you. We've been calling you for hours. Are you okay?"

"I'm as okay as I'm gonna be. I'm sorry if I scared you. I just needed some time by myself. I'm on my way to my mom's. Can you meet me over there?"

"I'm on my way, ma. I'll see you in a minute."

When I got to my mom's house, I could smell barbeque chicken and macaroni and cheese cooking as I walked up on the porch. I opened the door and she came rushing from the kitchen straight to me. She wrapped her arms around me as tight as she could and hugged me so tight I felt like I couldn't breathe.

"I'm so sorry, baby. I can't believe Mia's gone. She was like one of my own."

As she rocked me back and forth, I sobbed in her arms. "Why, Ma? Why Mia?"

"I don't know, baby, only God knows. She's in a better place though. She'll live through our memories and in our hearts. Everything's gonna be all right, sweetheart."

As she hugged me tighter, I wanted to believe her, but I knew deep down in my heart that wasn't true. It wasn't gonna be all right and things would never be the same.

I broke down crying in her arms as the thoughts of Mia raced through my mind. There was no more hiding the pain and trying to be strong for other people. Reality was starting to set in and it was emotionally more than I could handle. I wasn't ready yet, and the tears just kept flowing. My mom walked me upstairs to my old bedroom. "Take off your clothes and lay down. I'll be right back with something to help you sleep."

There was so much going on. I was mentally and emotionally exhausted. She knew my mind would keep racing and I wouldn't be able to sleep on my own, so she brought me two Xanax to help me calm down and rest. My phone was ringing non-stop, so she took my phone, pulled the covers over me, kissed me on the cheek, and told me to get some rest.

She closed the door just enough to make the room dark, but left it cracked, so she could hear me if I called her. I could see the hallway light peeking through the small slither of open space. It reminded me of the sun peeking through the clouds when the sky breaks after a rainy day. At first, I couldn't fall asleep. My brain was still working overtime. I had so many thoughts running through my mind, I was getting a headache. The two things I couldn't figure out was why and if I could've done anything that would've changed the course of events.

I kept thinking about Mia and what a good time we had today and how we were supposed to be on our way to the party right now. Instead I'm here, she's gone, and things would never be the same again. I started crying so hard that the whole right side of the pillow was soaking wet. Then, the pill started working and I drifted off to sleep.

When I woke up, I felt kind of groggy. It felt like I'd been sleeping for days. I walked over to the window and peaked through the blinds and saw that it was pitch black outside. After I used the bathroom, I washed my hands and splashed hot water on my face a couple of times, hoping to wash away the pain. It didn't work.

As I walked downstairs, my mom met me at the bottom.

"Are you okay, honey? Did you sleep okay?"

"Yeah Mom. I'm okay, I guess. What time is it?"

"It's late, honey. Do you want something to eat? Ty came to check on you, but you were sound asleep. He gave you a kiss and asked you to call him when you wake up."

"He did? I didn't even hear him come in the room. Where's my phone?"

"That thing wouldn't stop ringing. I finally figured out how to turn it off. It's in the kitchen," she said, laughing.

"Okay Mom, thanks."

As I walked in the kitchen to get my phone, she followed me.

"Are you hungry? I'll make you some breakfast."

"No, Ma. I'm not hungry. I'm still a little tired. I know Ty's worried about me, so I'm gonna go home and try to get some sleep."

"You're not leaving here this time of the night, so I can get a phone call about you next. Go back upstairs and lay back down for a little while. You're gonna need your rest and strength to deal with the next couple of days."

I was sad, tired, confused, and not up for an argument, so I text Ty to let him know I'd be home in the morning and went back upstairs to bed. When morning came, I woke up, got dressed, and left before my mom woke up. I didn't want her to worry about breakfast and all that. I didn't have an appetite anyway.

I needed to go by Mia's mom's house to talk to Kasey and I had to go home to talk to Ty. I wanted to go home and talk to Ty first, shower, and then get dressed. When I got home, he greeted me the same way my mom did— hugging me and asking me questions I didn't have the answers to.

I didn't want to cry, but I couldn't hold back the tears. He hugged me and rubbed my back. "Let it out, babe. Holding it in is only gonna hurt more."

"I can't get her out my head, Ty. I can't figure out why her. It's killing me."

"I know, babe. I know. This shit is crazy. She was too good of a person to go like that."

"I'm gonna get dressed and go to Kasey's and Mama Walker's to see if they heard anything from the cops."

He wiped my tears and gave me a kiss. As I grabbed my towel and headed for the shower, he looked at me with the cutest grin in the world and sarcastically asked, "Want some company?"

I laughed for the first time since I heard about Mia. "Not now, babe, but thanks for asking." As I walked in the bathroom, I smirked and thought to myself how much I loved Ty. I turned the water on as hot as I could stand it and got in. No music today, just me and my thoughts. I've been told several times that I tend to over think sometimes, but right now it's impossible not to.

☐

Chapter 4
Love Is Evil

After my shower, I got dressed, kissed Ty, and went to go meet Kasey. On my way to Mia's mom's house, I stopped at the deli we always went to and there were balloons, candles, pictures of Mia, and empty liquor bottles lining the front and sides of the store. Once again, reality smacked me in the face and it took everything in me to fight back the tears. There were people signing her pictures, putting flowers down, and lighting candles. Some were just staring at the whole scene in disbelief and shaking their heads.

As I walked up, all eyes were on me. Everybody knew wherever I was, Mia was. They were expecting me to break down, but I held it together as much as I could. I walked up, lifted my Ray Bans up, and just stood there for a minute staring at her pictures. Most of them I had already seen, but there was one of me, Mia, and Kasey on her twenty-first birthday. The picture made me cry, because we had so much fun together. Things would never be the same. I wiped my face and signed a couple

35

of pictures, and then I went in the store, got a ginger ale, and left.

I met Kasey at the mall. We shopped for our outfits for Mia's funeral and talked about everything that's been going on. We were both hearing the same things. It was crazy because things just weren't making sense. I bought a couple outfits for the yearly weekend getaway I was going on with my cousins this weekend. Even though I really don't want to go because I can't get my mind off Mia, it's a family tradition. My mom insists this is just what I need right now. Every year, all the females in my family over eighteen get together and go on a weekend getaway to bond and spend family quality time with each other. That's our way of staying close, because times are crazy. Any day one of us could be gone.

I spoke to Keys a couple of days ago. He agreed to take Mia's dog and keep her for the weekend while I went away with my family, because Ty had to work all weekend. So after I left the mall with Kasey, I picked up the dog and went to Keys' house to drop her off. I called him when I pulled up outside and he came outside to get her.

"Hey Keys. How you holdin' up?"

"I'm holdin' on, Tam, tryna maintain. Still keep thinking when I wake up I'm gonna roll over and she's gonna be right there next to me. Then, I open my eyes and I'm all alone. Shit hurts, Tam."

"Yeah, I know what you mean. I keep waiting to hear Nicki Minaj singing through my phone at least ten times a day, but I'm not getting those calls anymore."

We spoke about the arrangements for Mia's services and when and what time I'd be back to pick up the dog.

I could tell he was hurting and missing Mia because he looked like shit and reeked of Henney. He'd been drunk all day and night since Mia died. I tried to tell him all the liquor in the world couldn't make the pain go away, but he wasn't trying to hear it. He kept telling me how he couldn't sleep, so he drinks until he passes out.

I knew it was guilt eating him up, because one way or another, this had something to do with him. I just didn't know how yet. He wiped the tears from his face as we talked. He then took the dog out of the car and grabbed her overnight bag. "Okay Tammy, hit me when you get back. I'll meet you here," he said as he walked away.

"Okay Keys, thanks," I replied, then pulled off.

As I drove home, I tried to put together the pieces of the puzzle, but there were too many pieces missing. Who wanted Keys enough to kill Mia? Why not just kill Keys? Harsh as it sounds, if they wanted him, why go through her unless they were trying to send a message? I was completely confused but intent on figuring it out. I went home for a moment, and then met my cousins at my aunt's house.

While we were riding to Myrtle Beach, I had my headphones on listening to Mary J's My Life album on repeat, trying to zone out. However, the whole time in the back of my mind was the thought that when I get back home, I have to bury my best friend. Even still, I had a good time in Myrtle Beach with my family. I was feeling good half of the time, but the other half I felt depressed and distanced myself from everyone. While driving back, reality again hit me. I was on my way back home, back to the pain and chaos. The one thing I was looking forward to was seeing Ty, because I missed him. He always knew how to make me feel better.

When we got back, I hit Keys' phone, so I could pick up the dog on my way home. I knew Ty and I were gonna get it in, and then I was going to sleep. So, I figured I might as well take care of everything before I went home. Keys told me he was home about to get showered and dressed. He told me to hit his phone when I pulled up and he'd come open the door. I dropped my mom off and went to Keys' house.

As I walked up to the door, I called his phone and told him I was outside. About a minute later, he came down and opened the door for me in a towel.

"My bad, Tammy. I just got out the shower. I have to get dressed and go handle some things. Her bag and stuff is in the living room. Her bowls and food is in the kitchen."

"Okay thanks. I'll get her and her stuff together. Thanks again for keeping her while I was gone. I appreciate it."

"No problem, ma, anytime. I'm gonna go get dressed. Holla if you need me."

He walked in the bedroom to start getting ready. I started gathering the dog's belongings, but I couldn't find her leash. I looked around the living room and the dining room but I couldn't find it anywhere.

I walked in the kitchen to look for it. "Keys," I yelled. He came running out the bedroom in some boxers and a wife beater.

"What? What's wrong?"

"I can't find her leash. Have you seen it?"

"I thought it was in the living room. I'll help you find it."

We both looked around the apartment for a minute trying to find it. He walked in the kitchen to tell me he had found it. He stopped dead in his tracks, completely distracted by the sight of my ass as I was bent over cleaning up the dog food I knocked over in the kitchen. When I stood up and turned around, he was still staring and our eyes locked for a moment. That minute felt like eternity.

"You found it?" I asked, breaking the uncomfortable silence.

"Yeah, here you go," he replied as he walked towards me with the leash in his hand. I took the leash from his hand and turned to walk away and he grabbed my hand. He turned me back towards him and looked at me with sex in his eyes and kissed me. I don't know why I let him. I don't know why I didn't stop him. More importantly, I don't know why I kissed him back. It didn't stop with the kiss though. That was just the beginning.

He grabbed my other hand and I dropped the leash on the floor. Our fingers intertwined as he raised my arms and put them behind his neck. I pulled him closer to me and kissed him. I don't know what came over me. I didn't know I felt like that about Keys until that moment.

He lifted me up on the counter and started kissing me like he missed me. He erotically bit my bottom lip while his hand found its way inside my panties and started playing with my juice box. First, he inserted one finger to massage my throbbing clit, and then another... Before I knew it, he had me moaning, pulling him closer with one arm around his neck and the other gripping the underside of the counter. He slid his fingers in and out 'til my wet, sticky juices coated his fingers. He knew he had me already. This was just the appetizer. The main course solidified the fact that I'd be seeing him again.

He pulled down his black Polo boxer briefs, sliding me down on the counter, so that my ass was hanging off the edge. Then, he shoved his face in my honey pot. When his tongue touched my clit, my whole body warmed with pleasure. I gasped deeply and arched my back. It felt so good but so wrong at the same time. I knew I should've stopped, but I couldn't.

My fingers traced the smooth deep waves in his hair as he ate my pussy like it was his last meal. He gripped my thighs and pushed his tongue in and out as deep as it could go inside of me, taking time between strokes to twirl it around my clit before diving back in. I knew he could tell that he was driving me crazy by how wet I was. My fingers went from tracing his waves to palming the back of his head, pulling him closer while I lifted my ass off the counter to ride his tongue.

"Uhh, yes! Right there, don't stop," I begged as I fucked his face.

"Mmmm, this pussy so sweet," he moaned. "I can eat it all day." He lifted his face out my lap and kissed me with so much passion he had my heart damn near jumping out my chest. Then, he stepped back and started stroking himself with one hand and teasing me with the other. "See what you do to me?"

I spread my legs, draped my arms around his neck, and pulled him into me. When he slid in, it felt so good that I couldn't even breathe. My mouth hung open as he dug deeper and deeper inside me, pumping hard and fast.

I don't even know what he was saying to me. I was so caught up in the moment. I heard his voice but couldn't even focus on the words.

All I could say was "Yes! Harder! Damn, don't stop!" He had me so gone I would've agreed to anything as long as he didn't stop.

"Fuck, I'm 'bout to come," he shouted. He started fucking me so hard I almost fell off the counter.

"Shit, I'm coming," I let out as my body shook. My breath was entirely gone. He pumped faster and then he climaxed, too.

We leaned into each other and just stayed there for a minute, stuck in the moment. As I rode out my orgasm, my legs shook and my mind snapped back to reality. He kept kissing me in different places all over my body. As he paid special attention to my neck, my collar bone, and my shoulder, it sent chills shooting throughout my body. His lips were so soft that I nearly melted with each kiss. I knew I had to get out of there or I'd be in more trouble than I was already in.

I got up and started putting my clothes on and he kept trying to talk to me about what just happened, but I couldn't. I didn't know what to say or how to say it. All I knew was it was wrong on so many levels that I lost count. I never felt like that before, not even with Ty. That scared me.

I kissed him on the cheek. "I have to go."

"Damn, you gonna do me like that, Tam?"

"I can't stay here or I'm gonna fuck you again. I can't believe we just did that."

"Tammy, hold on. Slow down and let me talk to you for a minute." He pulled up his boxer briefs and followed me as I put my clothes on, grabbed the dog's stuff, and the dog.

"I can't, Keys. I'll call you later. I gotta go." He walked me down the stairs.

"A'ight Tam, I'll talk to you later." I walked to the car juggling the dog and her stuff, all while trying to keep myself together. I didn't have to turn around. I could feel him watching me.

As I drove home, our entire sex scene kept replaying in my mind. The sex was amazing and so passionate. I wanted more, but then I started thinking about Mia and the guilt set in. Damn, my best friend just died and I just fucked her boyfriend. That's about as disrespectful as it gets. That's the grimy type of shit the girls around the way did on a regular basis that we used to talk about. I can't believe I just cheated on Ty and disrespected Mia like that. I was an emotional mess and I didn't know what to do.

With all the shit Ty had done in the past, I've never cheated on him. Now that things were going good, I'm fucking up. While I wrestled with thoughts of guilt and regret, I drove home trying to figure out how to act normal. I couldn't let Ty find out what happened. What made it all worse was the fact that it was the best sex I'd ever had. I had never felt anything like the way he made me feel and I wanted more. It wasn't the forbidden fruit theory; it was just pure passion, pain, and pleasure. That's a dangerous combination.

I pulled up at my house, put the car in park, looked in the mirror, and gave myself a pep talk. "Damn Tammy, get it together. Walk in like nothing's wrong and do what you gotta do," I said. When I walked in, Ty was lying down on the couch watching the football game. I put the dog and my bags down and gave him a big hug and kiss. "Hey babe, I missed you," he said, pulling me down on top of him. He kept kissing me and squeezing my ass. I knew where he was going, but I also knew what I had just done with Keys. I couldn't let it go down like that.

I kept pausing in between kisses, telling him to wait a minute. Then, I got up off of him and stood up.

"Hold on, babe. I'm dirty and sweaty from the trip. Let me hop in the shower and get sexy for you."

"All right, hurry back. You woke him up and he's ready," he said, smiling with his hands in his sweats. I went in the bathroom, turned on my Chris Brown playlist, and got in the shower. I lathered up with more soap than usual, letting the steamy hot water beam onto my body, but all the soap in the world and holy water couldn't wash away my sins. I had to figure out a way to not have sex with Ty without making him suspicious.

So I got out the shower, put some sweats on, grabbed a bag of chips, sat down next to him on the couch, and started watching the game.

"Who's winning?" I asked.

"The Giants. Umm, what happened to something sexy?" He looked me up and down.

"I'm exhausted, babe. I just want to lay down and watch the game with you," I replied while wrapping the blanket around me. He always complained that we don't lay up and watch the games together like we used to, so I knew he'd fall for that. "Okay babe, but you're gonna have to share them covers though," he said, smiling and pulling on the covers. We layed up and watched the games until we both fell asleep.

The night of Mia's funeral was the first time Keys and I saw each other after what happened. We sat in the same row at her services. Ty was by my side the whole time. The guilt was eating me up. I was truly grieving and also feeling horrible for what I had done. When the services were over and we were all leaving, Keys gave Ty a hug, hugged me, and kissed me on the cheek, and then he left. It was an innocent gesture, but because of the guilt I was feeling, it felt awkward for me.

In the days that followed, I kept my distance from everyone except for Ty. I was so depressed all I did was work and stay home in the bed. Ty was worried about me, but he understood I was in a funk and having a hard time handling everything that was going on. Keys called my phone a couple of times, but I declined his calls and erased him from my call log. I didn't want Ty to find out he was calling, and I didn't want to talk about what had happened.

I guess I figured if I ignored the situation, it would go away, but it didn't. I was at work and Keys text me saying he needed to see me about something important. I agreed to meet him after work at Petco, because I had to pick up some things for the dog on my way home. When I pulled up in the front of Petco, he was already there sitting in his car waiting. I took a couple deep breaths, checked myself in the mirror, and gave myself a pep talk before I got out the car. "Keep it short and sweet, and get the fuck outta here and home to Ty," I told myself.

As I walked towards his car, he got out eyeing me from head to toe. I walked over to him and gave him a hug. I took a step back, leaned up against his car, and sat my Chanel bag on it.

"So, what's up? I been hitting your phone. What, you ducking my calls now?" he asked, smiling.

"I'm not ducking you. I just don't know what to say to you. I've been going through a lot lately. I'm going to be one hundred percent honest with you. What we did was wrong. It was about as wrong as wrong can get, but it was so good though. My head was already fucked up because of Mia, then that made it like ten times worse. I've never cheated on Ty. I honestly love him and don't want to lose him."

"I can respect that. I don't know what came over me. Since we're being honest right now, I've always had feelings for you. Don't get me wrong. I loved Mia. She was my heart, but I was always attracted to you. Crazy thoughts crossed my mind sometimes, but I just never acted on them. I never wanted to hurt Mia and I didn't want to fuck things up with you and Ty, so I kept it to myself.

When you were at my place looking all sexy and we were alone, I couldn't help it. I just couldn't let you walk out without showing you what's been on my mind."

I couldn't believe what he was saying to me. I was trying to keep a poker face and not show any emotion while he was talking, but it was hard. I was going crazy inside. I knew where this was headed, so I had to cut this short and get out of there before we made another mistake.

"I appreciate your honesty and you sharing your feelings with me, but just like Mia was your heart, she was mine, too. So is Ty. I'm not gonna lie, the sex was crazy, but we both know we can't continue that situation. I don't think it's a good idea for us to be alone anymore, because things may get out of hand. That's not gonna be good for either of us."

I picked up my bag off his car and gave him a hug.

"I'll see you around, Keys," I said as I turned and walked away.

"Wow Tammy, just like that, huh? I hate to see you leave, but I love to watch you go," he said and laughed as I walked away. I turned around and smiled at him, then I got in my car and pulled off.

I put my Jeezy Tm: 103 CD on super loud in the car, and drove for about five minutes before my phone rang. It was Keys. "Meet me at the Marriott. I'm on my way there right now," he said in a sexy but demanding voice. He caught me completely off guard.

I turned Jeezy down and replied, "Huh?"

"Tammy, stop playing with me. You know you want it like I want it. I could see it in your face when we were talking. Now stop wasting time and get your ass to the Marriott. When you get to the desk tell them you're with me. They'll tell you the room number." Just like that, he hung up the phone and my mind started spinning. Once again, I knew it was wrong, but something was pulling me towards him.

I stopped at the red light, lost in deep thought. I was thinking so hard, I forgot I was at the light. The car behind me started laying on the horn, jolting me back to reality. I debated with myself, go home like I should, make dinner, and have a nice night with Ty. Or, go meet Keys like I want and get what my body's screaming for, even though I know it's wrong. My heart was fighting with my thoughts and my heart lost. I went to the Marriott to meet Keys...

I got to the front desk and did what he said. The attendant gave me the room key along with a look that let me know she knew what I was there for. I went up to the room. When I opened the door, to my surprise, there was a girl sitting on the couch texting. Keys was walking around on the phone with a drink in his hand. He cut his phone conversation short, walked over to me, kissed me on the cheek, and then introduced me to his friend.

"Tammy, this is my friend, Mani. Mani, this is Tammy." She waved and replied, "Hey hon." As he introduced us, I was trying to figure out why he called me to come here. Who was this chick, Mani? What was she about and who did she know? She didn't seem like the rowdy type. She had a pretty mocha complexion, nice body, and long, black wavy hair that rested on her chest like an accessory to her accessories. She wasn't being ratchet, wasn't yelling, or being ignorant. She was laying back on the black leather couch texting and periodically paying attention to us. But nobody was supposed to know that Keys and I were messing around.

"Want a drink?" Keys asked while lifting his glass.

"No I'm good, thanks." I sat my bag down on the table and took my jacket off. He came up behind me and started kissing on my neck then whispered in my ear.

"She's cool. We fuck around, but we do our thing. She knows I fuck with you and wants to watch." He completely mind-fucked me. I wasn't used to this type of situation. Normally girls wanted to fight and act crazy, so I was shocked yet slightly intrigued. She was comfortable enough with herself and their situation to explore her fantasy. Apparently, I fitted in with their situation nicely.

He put his arm around my waist and sat his drink down on the table next to my bag. I closed my eyes and let my body feel the full effect of his soft lips gliding across the back of my neck as his hands explored my thighs. He was wearing Gucci Guilty cologne. I love a good-smelling man. That combined with what he was doing to me was turning me on like crazy. Again, he had me totally out of character. I guess he could sense my hesitation, so he turned me around. We were now standing face to face. He kissed me slowly, softly, and seductively, all while unbuttoning my jeans.

"Relax, ma. I got you. You trust me, right?" he asked in between kisses.

I kissed him back. "What you think?" I replied while holding his face and kissing him.

He lifted my shirt up over my head, got down on his knees, and started kissing my stomach. I ran my fingers through his hair and glanced over at Mani. She was laying on the couch watching. She kept eye contact with me while he kissed on my stomach and thighs, all while taking my clothes off, piece by piece.

This felt different. I got a rush knowing somebody was watching and becoming aroused. It brought something out of me that made me want to perform. He layed me down on the bed, spread my legs apart, and laid between them. I could tell by how he was grinding on me while sucking my nipples that he wanted it as bad as I did. His soft lips slowly worked their way down my body. Once again, Keys had me caught up in the moment, kissing and licking my sweet spot.

Then, I felt another soft wet set of lips kissing on my neck as he played in my pussy. I opened my eyes and it was Mani. She stopped kissing my neck and leaned over me so we were face to face. She kissed me real slow and deep it took my focus off what Keys was doing. She caught me off guard, but I was pleasantly surprised. Our long, deep kiss shook me to the core. She kissed me like she meant it, like she had something to prove. I'd never been kissed like that. My heart raced and my whole body ignited with passionate fire.

I could smell the soft, sweet scent of her perfume as our tongues twirled around each other. She sucked my tongue and bottom lip. I felt my body reacting, I was getting wetter and wetter. She broke the kiss and worked her way down to my nipples. Then I felt Keys stop. I looked to my right and he was taking his clothes off, watching as Mani picked up where he left off. Her lips created an erotic trail down my body, sending tremors throughout my entire being every time her lips made contact with my skin. She looked up at me as she kissed, slurped, and played with my pretty kitty.

Her lips were soft and warm. I was going crazy inside but trying to play it cool. What she was doing to my body was making me dizzy. I'd never been with a girl before. I didn't see a problem with being gay or lesbian, but it just wasn't my thing. Mani was so pretty though with her alluring eyes, deep dimples, long silky hair, perky tits, and plump ass. Who could say no to that? She was so good at what she was doing. I didn't want her to stop, and she didn't. She kissed my juice box like she kissed my lips. Then, she slid her two fingers in and out slowly while sucking and biting on my inner thigh.

"You like that?" she asked

"Mhmm," I moaned as she pulled her fingers out, licked my juices off, flashed me the sexiest smile, and went back to pleasing me.

Keys walked up behind Mani, grabbed her by the waist, pulled her down toward the edge of the bed, and spread her legs. He played with her clit for a minute until she was wet and moaning with her face in mine. He smacked her ass and asked, "You ready for me?" Without waiting for an answer, he slid inside her and pumped in and out with long, deep strokes while she sucked and licked on me.

They were both blowing my mind. He started fucking her harder. I could hear her ass smacking against him as he pounded her while pulling her hair and looking at me. The harder he went, the wilder she got. Then, we switched positions. I got on top and rode him. She sat on his face. He ate her while she kissed me. She caressed my face with her perfectly painted nails, moaning, kissing me, and swirling her tongue around mine. She was bringing out things in me I didn't even know existed.

I got up off him, turned around, and rode him in a reverse cowgirl position as she layed down in front of me. They had me so caught up I didn't even think twice before I kissed and slurped her pretty pussy. It was soft, warm, wet and sweet. She closed her eyes and squirmed, trying not to lose control as her warm juices filled my mouth.

"Mmmm yes," she moaned.

It was my first time, but you couldn't tell by how she was moaning, squirming, and gripping my hair with both hands. He was smacking my ass, grinding to the rhythm of my body.

I don't know what came over me, but the two of them were the perfect combo, and they had me about to lose it. I could tell Mani was ready to come. Her back arched up off the bed and she got wetter while I blew and sucked on her clit, snaking my tongue back and forth. "Yeah, like that. Right there, don't stop. Damn, I'm 'bout to come," she moaned in total ecstasy. Just when I felt her about to explode, I stopped, turned around, and told Keys, "She want it." I got up off him and he slid up in her, giving it to her hard and fast until she came.

She lay on the bed exhausted and watched him bend me over the bed and stroke me from the back until we both came. Then, the three of us passed out in the bed. I woke up a couple hours later in the bed between the two of them. Keys was knocked out and Mani had her arm draped over my waist knocked out, too. As I moved to get up, Mani woke up looked at me for a second and fell back asleep. I got dressed, kissed them both, and left.

Chapter 5
Life on the Rocks

My life was getting hectic. I was trying to balance my relationship with Ty, my secret situation with Keys, working, and kicking it with Kasey. She and I became a lot closer after Mia died. We were always close. We were like the three musketeers, but now that there were only two of us left, we grew closer than ever. I found myself becoming a different person. I never used to lie before. Now I was doing it often and getting good at it. I never used to cheat. Now I was doing that quite often and getting good at that, too. I felt like nothing was the same anymore and neither was I. I'd been seeing Keys on the side for a couple months and it was getting crazy. We were sneaking off having sex any and everywhere.

He was like a drug, and I was addicted. He had no problem letting me know the feeling was mutual; neither of us wanted it to stop. Ty thought I was spending more time with Kasey and had no clue I was cheating, because I still loved him and never treated him any different. I never knew I had it in me to be able to do some of the things I was doing. I truly was becoming a different person and living a double life. Kasey suspected something was up with me, but wasn't sure exactly what it was. I was extra careful with my actions, because I couldn't let her get even the slightest inkling that I was dealing with Keys or my life would be over.

In the days that followed, I continued my day-to-day activities like nothing ever happened. Ty, Kasey, and I went to the bike show at the Jacob Javits Center. Normally Ty went with his boys and Me, Mia, and Kasey went together, but this year everything was different. I gave Kasey my phone to take a picture of me on a Can Am and as she was taking the picture, a friend request and message popped up.

She handed the phone to me. "You have a message in your notifications, Tam. Who's Ms. Mani?" she asked. I almost choked on my Fiji water. My mind scrambled for a quick response, "Friend of a friend," I responded as I quickly changed the subject and walked over to the next section of bikes. As we walked and checked out the bikes, my mind kept switching gears from what I did the other day to who I was with right now. We enjoyed our afternoon taking pictures, Instagramming, Facebooking, and putting pictures on Twitter. After lunch, we hit the turnpike and headed back home.

The whole way home, Mani and I were inboxing back and forth on Facebook. I kind of got the feeling she was trying to get to know me. After that night with her and Keys, I was definitely a little intrigued, too. We exchanged numbers and started texting. It was crazy though, because how we met felt different than how our conversations went. When we talked, it was completely non-sexual. Over the course of a couple days, we spoke and text a lot. It wasn't forced conversation. It just flowed and felt very natural. We clicked, and because she knew everything about me and Keys secret situation, I could talk to her about things I couldn't talk to anyone else about.

We both were still seeing him, so we grew comfortable with each other. We would talk to each other about him. I even talked to her about Ty and how I was caught in between the two and still feeling guilty for doing this to Mia. She even seemed to understand how I missed her. I finally got everything off my chest. It felt like ten pounds of pressure was lifted, and I could finally breathe again. She met me in a crazy way, at a fucked up time in my life, and somehow, more than anybody else, she understood me.

Kasey was feeling the distance between us. One day she hit me up to do lunch, so I met her at Bahama Breeze. We sat down and started catching up on what had been going on.

"What's up with you and Ty? I haven't seen you two in like two weeks. Y'all don't know me anymore, huh?" she asked and laughed.

"We've both been working a lot and I've been back in the gym trying to get my mind and body right. Shit still doesn't feel right yet, but I guess reality is setting in."

"Yeah, I know. I still think about her every day. I keep wishing it was all a bad dream, but I know it's not. You ain't been around to help me occupy my mind. I think I'm gonna start hitting the gym with you, Tammy. That might help."

"Let's get it then, shit. We're in there tomorrow morning."

"Yup, call me when you get up. I'll meet you over there." We finished our lunch, and then I went to meet Keys at the Breaker Hotel.

That was our getaway spot, on the beach in Spring Lake. It had beautiful rooms, a beautiful view, and nobody we knew even knew about it. The staff was familiar with us and took care of us every time we came. We ordered room service, and I went in the bathroom to start the Jacuzzi. I never told Keys that Mani and I were getting close. He didn't even know we had spoken and seen each other since that night.

Rose', red lighting, and Trey Songs on my Beats Pill speakers set the mood right. I felt like showing him that soft sexy side of me that I usually reserve for Ty, so I set everything up, climbed in the Jacuzzi, and called him to come in the bathroom. I had it looking like a video scene. After the third time of calling his name with no response, I got anxious and got out to see what he was doing.

As I walked out the bathroom in a towel still talking to him and getting no answer, I realized why. He was stretched across the bed knocked out. I just looked at him for a minute in disbelief, mad because I was horny, tipsy, and looking stunning with no one to appreciate it. I got my phone, took a picture of him sleeping, and sent it to Mani with the caption, They usually fall asleep after not before. She text me back, Lol, now what?

I told her I was going home. I knew Ty was still up and would gladly relieve my frustrations. She told me she was at Friday's not far from my house. She invited me to come by and have a drink first, to relax a little, and then go home and give it to Ty. I agreed and told her I'd be there in twenty minutes. Little did I know, once again my life was about to change forever.

We had a couple of drinks and decided to take a ride in my car. I was driving while my Fabulous Soul Tape 3 cd played. She leaned over, sucked on my earlobe, and blew in my ear. She slowly kissed her way down my neck while her hand traveled across my thigh and found its way to the button on my True Religion jeans.

I kept my eyes on the road while the rest of my body reacted to her. My nipples were so hard they were poking through my bra pressing against my shirt. With every kiss, I became wetter. Like she could sense my anticipation, she lifted my shirt, pulled my bra to the side, and sucked my nipples, giving each one special attention. My pussy was throbbing and my body was craving her. She never said a word, so I did.

"Damn Mani, what you trying to do to me?"

"What you want me to," she replied with a sexy laugh and a kiss.

I could taste the peach Ciroc on her tongue. The liquor was present but not overpowering. Her kisses were intoxicating, reminding me of our last encounter and how good she tasted. This time, there was no Keys, just us. As her lips made their way down my body, I forgot all about Keys and Ty; it was just us and that was just fine. As she unbuttoned my jeans, I lifted my ass off the seat and she pulled them down past my knees.

My panties were soaked, so she pulled them to the side and flicked her middle finger up and down on my clit until it was throbbing. My juices coated her finger. Then, she slid two fingers in and out, fucking me with her fingers. When I started grinding to her strokes, she knew she had me. "You like that, babe? You like my fingers inside of you?" she asked while speeding up the strokes.

I moaned as I sped up to match her rhythm. "Yes baby, right there. Don't stop. Oh my god, you got me so wet right now, but I don't wanna come yet." As I said that, she pulled her two fingers out and buried her face in between my thighs. She wrapped her lips around my clit and sucked while flicking her tongue back and forth.

"Oh shit! Damn Mani, what the fuck? You're gonna make me crash." My words were mixed with moans as I took one hand off the wheel and gripped her neck with it.

She stopped sucking my clit and softly kissed every part of my pussy, pausing in between each kiss to tell me how good it tastes. "Mmmm, she's so wet, sticky, and sweet like pineapple." Then, she quickly slid her tongue in and stroked me with it like it was a dick. I had never felt anything like that before and found myself wondering why Ty and Keys couldn't make me feel like that.

She had that special touch. I didn't have to prompt her, guide her, or tell her what I liked. She just knew what to do, and did it so good that I couldn't take it. I tried to hold back my orgasm, but she felt my pussy throbbing, gripping, and releasing her tongue with every stroke. As my foot involuntarily pressed down on the gas pedal, I worked the wheel with one hand while holding her in a neck lock, stuffing her face in my pussy.

If I was hurting her, she didn't let on. She just kept going. The faster the car went, the faster her tongue went. The engine was racing and so was my heart. In between short, quick breaths I uttered, "I'm about to come." As I fucked her face, her nails dug into my thigh. She pulled her tongue out and sucked my clit until I came. As my juices flowed, she slurped and swallowed while my legs shook. Finally, my grip on her neck lightened up.

I dropped her off and headed to my house once again replaying our episode in my head. It was something special about her. She was all in my head and working her way into my heart. I never knew another female could have that effect on me. I'd never even considered being with a woman before, but now I was finding myself wanting her more than Keys. What's crazy was the fact that he had no idea we're messing around. I love Ty and was definitely not leaving him, but I couldn't keep cheating on him with both of them. It was too much to handle. It's a delicate dance replacing your side piece with their side piece, but it was time to tango.

?

?

Chapter 6
Shall We Dance

It was Ty's birthday and he decided he wanted to spend the weekend in Atlantic City. So, I reserved a Jacuzzi room for us at Harrah's and set up a sexy weekend for us to show him how much I loved him. Due to my recent activities, guilt made me feel like I needed to go the extra mile to keep things right with Ty. He had no idea what my motivation was. He just loved the special attention. We went to Ruth's Chris for dinner, which was one of my favorite spots. After a great meal and a couple shots of Louis XIII, we hit the crap tables. He did his thing with the dice while I drank Ciroc and Sprite and text with Mani.

She wanted to see me, but I couldn't and I explained to her why. Then, she hit me with an indecent proposal. She wanted a threesome with me and Ty. I was completely caught off guard by the offer and almost choked on my drink as I read the text. She went on about what a great birthday surprise that would be for him and how he would love me even more for exploring other avenues with him sexually. It took a minute to digest. She completely mind-fucked me.

What we did with Keys was one thing, but my relationship with Ty was a different story. I hesitated to respond, but she didn't hesitate to push for it. Her texts were coming faster than I could read them. As I watched Ty throw the dice, I thought about how he would react to me and Mani all over him and all over each other. Thinking about it was turning me on. I hit Mani back and told her I was with it, to get herself together, and get out here.

Ty gambled a little more, and then went to Caesar Mall to watch the water show and do a little shopping. I had to stall him a little until Mani got here and set things up. I text her specific instructions on how I wanted things to be set up in the room, so I could make it real sexy for him. When we got back to the room, I saw she'd done everything exactly as I asked. Ty loved it. "Aww, you did this for me? Thanks, babe." He gave me a big hug and kiss. She put rose pedals everywhere and had red honeysuckle nectar candles strategically placed in areas around the room.

In the middle of the bed was a bucket full of ice with Moet Rose' and Bel Air Rose'. We kissed for a moment, and then I told Ty to chill and pop the Rose' while I got the Jacuzzi ready. He had no idea Mani was in the bathroom waiting for us. I hooked my phone up to my

Beats Pill, turned Pandora on. Then, I went in the bathroom and shut the door behind me.

Mani had the bathroom looking so sexy, and she was the perfect accessory. She was sitting on the counter in front of the mirror by the sink sipping champagne in a sexy ass black lace bra and thong. Her breasts sat up so pretty and perky like they were waiting to be touched. I could see myself kissing, sucking them, and working my way down her abs with my tongue. The candles provided the perfect lighting and atmosphere. I walked over to her and gave her a kiss. She broke the kiss and whispered, "Does he like it?" I whispered back, "Yes girl, he loves it and so do I.

Let me start the Jacuzzi," I said as I turned the water on and poured the bubbles in. She turned the switch on that activated the jets. As the Jacuzzi filled with water, I sat on the edge and watched as she stripped out of her bra and panties real slow and sexy for me. I told her to get in and I would bring Ty in and we could surprise him. She stood in front of me completely naked, with a glass of champagne in one hand and some beads wrapped around her other hand. Her hair and makeup were flawless.

She looked like a model. Her confidence and smile made her even more appealing. She leaned over like she was gonna kiss me and stopped just before our lips touched and whispered, "Don't keep me waiting." She was so sexy and had no idea how much she was turning me on.

Then she kissed me, took a step back, sipped the champagne, and let the beads dangle from her hand. "I'll be right back," I whispered as I turned off the water and walked out the bathroom.

I walked back in the room and Ty was sitting on the bed drinking Rose' from the bottle with his shirt off. He was on his phone Instagramming. My brain shifted gears and my eyes instantly sized him up. He looked so sexy sitting there like that. I wanted to jump on him and ride him until we both came, but I had to remember Mani was in the bathroom. I still had to get him in there. So, I crawled across the bed and straddled him. I grabbed the bottle of Rose' and took a sip. Then, I took his phone and snapped a picture of me sitting on him with the Rose' and posted it on his Instagram.

We started laughing, "Let them talk. Gotta feed the fish," I said laughing and kissed him. He laughed too and kissed me back. "You're crazy." As we kissed, he took my shirt off and unbuttoned my jeans. Before he could take them off, I stood up and grabbed his hand and stood him up, too. I slowly stepped out of my jeans and was down to my bra and panties.

I kissed his lips and his chest, and then unbuttoned his jeans and slid them off him until he was down to his Ethika boxer briefs. He was ready. I could see the bulge in his briefs waiting to be unleashed. I took his hand and started walking him towards the bathroom.

"I have something for you."

"Oh yeah, something like what?" he asked just before we walked into the bathroom.

I opened the bathroom door and walked him in. Mani was sitting in the Jacuzzi sipping champagne as candles glowed all around the Jacuzzi. "Ty, this is Mani. Mani this is Ty." I was nervous, but Ty's face was priceless. Mani was cool enough for the both of us though. That was one of the things I loved about her. I did things with her I didn't do with anyone else. She had a way of making everything work.

She stood up in the hot tub as water and bubbles ran down her beautiful body. She stepped out, walked up to Ty, and kissed him on the cheek.

"I'm Mani. I'm a good friend of Tammy's. I'm gonna help her show you a good time tonight for your birthday."

"Oh yeah?" he said and started laughing.

"This ain't real, Tammy. You ain't bout this." He obviously had no idea what I had been about lately, but tonight I was gonna show him. I turned to Mani, caressed her face, and gave her a slow deep kiss. She stepped into it, so we were chest to chest with our breasts pressed against each other. Next, she grabbed my ass and squeezed it.

Ty stood there watching as we kissed and fondled each other. She took my bra off and started sucking my nipples. They were so hard that they ached. Her kisses made them throb. Then, Ty joined her. He had one side and she had the other. Then, they kissed each other. Mani stopped and walked me over to the edge of the Jacuzzi. She sat me down, pulled my panties down, spread my legs, and admired the view. "Pretty ass pussy," she said as she licked her lips, and then kissed and slurped my kitty.

I leaned back and let her have her way with me. I watched Ty watching us and stroking his love muscle at the same time.

My hands got lost in her hair as she sucked and nibbled on my clit. Ty continued to stroke his dick while watching us. Mani stopped for a second and called Ty over. She slid her finger in and out my pussy until my juices were all over her finger, then she licked it off and kissed Ty. She was playing with my pussy with one hand and stroking his dick with the other.

Then, she pushed Ty's head down in my pussy and held it there as he twirled his tongue around my clit and forced it in and out with her assistance. I was so turned on I couldn't hold in my moans and screams. She stared me in my eyes the whole time he was eating my pussy, all while talking shit to me. This was turning me on even more. "Yeah, you like that shit, huh? Got his tongue all in that pussy. Get that shit! Mmmm, come here, papi. Let me taste it," she said as she lifted his head up and kissed him. Then, Mani put his face back in it.

She lifted his head up and unwrapped the beads from around her wrist, sliding them one by one in my pussy, taking time out to lick, kiss, and suck in between each bead. Ty came up behind her and slid his thick nine inches up in her. She stopped licking me for a second, gasped, and let a long moan out. "Uhhh!" I guess she wasn't anticipating the dick being that good, but she quickly adjusted. Ty loved it. He was long stroking her and smacking her ass, all while watching her play in my pussy with the beads and her tongue.

I didn't want to come yet, so I made her stop. We all got up and got in the Jacuzzi with the bottle of Rose'. He poured the drink on me and Mani and we slurped it off each other. Then he got in the middle and we all kissed each other. This felt different than when I was with Mani and Keys. It felt right and I felt the passion from her and Ty. I sat Ty back, got on top, and rode him while Mani and I kissed. Then, she got out and stood over him, put her hands on the wall to brace herself and sat on his face while he ate her pussy. Watching his face in her pussy and hearing her moaning made me ride him faster and faster until I couldn't take it anymore.

Water and bubbles were splashing everywhere and I was screaming and coming all over him. He felt it, gripped my ass with both hands, and fucked me harder than he'd ever fucked me before. I climbed off of him and Mani hopped back in the Jacuzzi and started riding Ty. I got behind her, grabbed her ass and waist, and helped her bounce up and down on him while smacking her ass. Then, he picked her up, turned her around, put her back against the wall, and gave it to her hard and fast as she locked her hands behind his neck. Her tits bounced every time their bodies collided.

Then, she couldn't take it anymore and was screaming, "I'm coming! What the fuck? Damn, don't stop!" He went harder and harder until he was about to come, too, "Yo, I'm about to come," He said as he pulled out and sat up on the edge of the Jacuzzi. We both got down in front of him she took one side and I took the other and sucked it together until he couldn't hold it in anymore and released his load in our mouths. We slurped it up and kissed each other as he lay back and watched.

She paused for a second, "See what I do for you?"

She kissed me again. That was the moment I realized we were more than friends... I was falling for her.

After Atlantic City, things changed between me and Mani. We were closer than ever, but she was also getting possessive. Things changed between Ty and I as well. He was also getting possessive and very curious. He started asking me questions about Mani and how close we were—questions I really didn't want to answer. Mani on the other hand wasn't worried about me and Ty. She knew I wouldn't leave Ty, but she wanted me to end things with Keys. She said he was no good for either of us and I needed to end it and so would she. Honestly, I'd lost interest in the whole situation with Keys anyway and had plans on ending things not because she wanted me to, but because I was over it. If it would make her feel better to think it was because of her, so be it.

I needed someone to talk to about the Mani/Ty situation, so I sat down with Kasey and told her what was going on minus Keys, because that was something I was prepared to take to the grave. We sat down outside at Uva Lounge in Bradley Beach and had drinks.

"So, I have a lot going on Kase and I need to talk to you."

"I haven't seen you in like two weeks. What's up? Is everything okay with you and Ty?"

"I know. I've been a little bit of everywhere lately. I apologize for the distance, but I'm caught up in some shit, Kase. I'm just gonna come out and say it. I had a threesome with Ty and Mani in A.C. for his birthday, and now I'm caught up between them."

"Oh wow! How'd that come about, and what you gonna do now?"

"I wanted to do something special for him. It was her idea, I agreed, and we all liked it. I've never liked something so much in my life. That shit was amazing, Kase. I still think about it from time to time. But now he's asking me all kinds of questions about me and her. And now she wants more of me and her. I love Ty, but I'd be lying if I said I wasn't feeling her, too.

I don't wanna cheat on Ty, but I can't stop fucking with her. It's something about her. She gets me in a way no one else does. She touches me in a way no one else does, and I just can't walk away right now."

"Wow, Tammy. I've never heard you talk like this before. She must've really done her thing. You shared Ty with her and y'all two fucked around? Where the fuck have I been?"

Shut up, Kase. You know I've never been with a girl before. She's just so different. I can't explain it. We have something different. I'm not leaving Ty, but honestly, I'm not ready to let go of Mani either."

"So, I guess I don't need to ask how it was. Obviously it was beyond good, because she's got you going."

"It was unbelievable, Kase. I wish we could do it just like that again, but I'm not sure what to do now. I don't know if I'm honest with Ty how he'll take it or if I should just do what I do with her and keep it between us two. I'm just scared it will come out later and I don't want to fuck up things with Ty."

"I don't know, Tam. What I do know is you need to be careful. She seems to have a hold on you and she might have one on Ty next."

"Yeah, I hear you, but I'm not worried about that. She only fucked with him for me. She's more into me than anyone else, trust me."

"If you say so... Just watch yourself and your man, too. Never underestimate people."

"I know. I'm on it. Thanks Kase, I just needed to vent with someone I can trust."

"You know I got you, always."

I drove home thinking about everything between Ty, Keys, Mani, and myself. I'd been ignoring Keys' texts and phone calls for days thinking it would make him go away, but it was just the opposite. Finally, I text him and told him I couldn't do this anymore and we had to go our separate ways. I told him Ty and I were starting to talk about marriage and I didn't want to mess things up. At first he agreed, but things would soon change. Mani and I got closer by the day and she stopped messing with Keys, too.

She started coming around a little more. Ty was okay with it. I told him there was nothing going on between Mani and I other than what happened that night. We were just good friends and I liked having her around, and he was cool with it. Truth was, we were getting closer than ever and I couldn't let her go. She made me feel what he didn't, she did the things he wouldn't, and most of all, we connected on a level no one else would understand. Kasey started to come back around a little more often after our talk, and I sensed the discomfort when she, Mani, and I were together.

One day, Kasey and I were alone and she told me I needed to cut Mani loose or at least fall back a little from the situation, because she felt like Mani was trying to take Mia's place. It sounded crazy to me when she said it. I was so blinded by my feelings I didn't even think twice about it. Ty and I were good, work was good, and Mani and I were exploring each other sexually on a regular basis, but nobody knew. To everyone else we were girls, friends, and homies, but we knew what it really was and the fact that no one knew made it even better.

⏥

Chapter 7
It Is What It Is

Keys saw some pictures Mani and I posted on her Instagram and realized that neither one of us were dealing with him anymore, but we were still dealing with each other. He was pissed off. He sent Mani a text asking her to meet him at his house to talk about something important. He sent me a text to call him, stating that it was important. I ignored and deleted the text. I was done with Keys and there was nothing else to talk about. I guess that wasn't gonna fly with him, because as I walked out my front door, I stopped mid-stride when I noticed Keys parked in front of my house.

I walked up to the passenger side and he rolled the window down.

"Hey, pretty girl. Where you headed?" I leaned in the window and pulled my shades up, so he could see my eyes.

"Keys, what are you doing here? Are you crazy? What if Ty comes home and sees you out here?"

"Well, if you answered your phone, I wouldn't be here right now, and you wouldn't be worrying about Ty. You and Mani are real cute in those pictures. Funny I haven't seen you two in a while, but I see y'all are getting along well."

"Yeah, we're good, Keys. How can I help you?"

"You know how you can help me. Meet me at my house, so I can show you how much I miss fucking you, licking you until you come, hitting it from the back, smacking your ass, and digging deep up in it," he said, licking his lips and grabbing his dick "I know you miss me."

"Keys, we never should've started. We both knew we were wrong. I can't keep doing that to myself, Ty, or Mia. I think we should keep our distance for a while and maybe one day we can be cordial. I just don't want any problems."

"Oh yeah, Tammy? You think shit's just that easy, huh? Well, I think if you want to keep things sweet with you and Ty, you and Mani better meet me at my house at nine o'clock tonight or I'm telling Ty everything. Oh and keep the pussy, ma; this is business. Tell ya' girl Mani I'm not playing with y'all either. Nine o'clock or I'm gonna shake up your world and hers, too." I stood there speechless as he rolled the window up and sped off.

I pulled my phone out, called Mani, and told her what had just happened. She told me she'd be over right after work and we could figure things out. I hung up the phone, went in the house, and poured a glass of D'usse straight on ice. I paced around the kitchen sipping and trying to figure out what the hell Keys wanted from us besides sex and how the hell I was going to get out of this without losing Ty. My mind was racing a million miles a minute, so I drank a little more, cleaned up the house, and started dinner. I had to occupy my mind until Mani came over to keep my mind busy. Mani finally got to the house and we sat down to figure things out.

"So, what do think he wants from us, Mani?"

"I don't know, but I guess we're going to find out. He text me a couple of times wanting to talk, but I've been blowing him off."

"Yeah, me too. Well, let's go together around eight thirty and get this shit over with. I'll tell Ty we're going to pick Kasey up from somewhere. She'll cover for us," I suggested while sipping my second glass of D'usse.

"Sounds good. I'm going to go home to shower and change. Call me when you're on your way."

"Okay." I walked her to the door, she gave me a kiss, and she left.

I finished fixing Ty dinner and put his plate in the microwave for him. He was working late, so I knew I wouldn't see him before I left. I took a shower, got dressed, and headed over to Mani's. I text Kasey on my way to Mani's in order to get her to cover for me. When I told her it was something I had to handle with Mani and I really couldn't discuss it, she wasn't happy about it and expressed her concerns, but she agreed. I picked Mani up and we headed to Keys' house. I text him and told him we were outside and he said the door was open come in.

When we walked in, he was sitting on the couch having a drink.

"Come in, ladies. Have a seat. It's good to see y'all. I see you have kept in touch. It's kind of crazy that I'm the one out of the loop when I brought you two together, but whatever, pussy is pussy. There's a million more of y'all." He laughed and sipped his drink.

"Okay, so why are we here, Keys?" Mani asked.

"Look at you, all business today, huh? That's cool. Time is money, so let's get down to business. I have a problem that y'all are going to help me solve."

"Oh yeah? What kind of problem?" I asked.

"I owe some pretty big people some pretty big money, and y'all are gonna help me make that problem go away."

"How is that our problem and why should we help you with anything?" I asked.

"If you want your life to stay happy and healthy, you'll do as I say. Mani, let's not forget how we met and how quickly I can pour salt on old wounds. Y'all help me and I let you live. I won't leak the pictures and video I have of y'all and won't alert the important people in your lives about your unsavory activities. We will all live happily ever after."

Mani and I traded glances, trying to read each other and figure out what to do or say. You could feel the tension in the room as Mani broke the uncomfortable silence.

"So what do you want us to do?"

"I'm going to rob Peter to pay Paul. There's these two guys, Jason and Pop, and they rubbed one of my affiliates the wrong way, so we're going to take care of them.

They're gun runners. They sell large quantities of guns in various states. They also tend to post up in strip clubs for hours at a time a couple times a week. They're at Jersey Girls every Sunday, so you two are going to get their attention and get them to leave with you and text me from where y'all are, so I can come through with my hittas and take them out. My affiliates will appreciate it, because they will take over their customers. I will appreciate it, because they will pay me, and I can pay my debt and live. Then, y'all will go back to life as you know it like nothing ever happened, and we're all good."

"You want us to set somebody up to die?" I asked.

"And why us? Why not some bout it bitches off the street that don't give a fuck?" Mani chimed in.

"Because it has to be someone I can trust that I know won't talk. Since you both stand to lose a lot if you talk, I figure you'll keep your mouths shut. Look, the guys I owe don't play and they're gonna kill the people close to me one by one until they get they're money. Y'all are in the line of fire, so I suggest you cooperate. Then, I can get them they're money, this shit can be over, and we can go our separate ways."

I didn't know what to say or do. I couldn't believe I had gotten myself into some shit like this.

Mani sat there with a poker face not saying a word, so I spoke for both of us.

"When is all of this supposed to go down?"

"I'll text you their pictures. We're gonna make it happen this Sunday."

"After this, I don't ever want to hear from you or see you again Keys," Mani said while glaring at him.

I stood up and motioned for Mani to come on. "All right, Keys, it is what it is. Send the pictures and let's get this over with, but I'm with Mani after this I don't know you." He smiled and as we walked out he followed us to the door.

"I'll be in touch, ladies."

We left Keys' house and headed back to Mani's. I pulled up and put the car in park. We sat there in silence for a minute as I gazed out the window. All of the sudden, it hit me like a ton of bricks.

"These guys had something to do with Mia," I said to Mani.

"They killed Mia, and if we don't figure something out, we could be next."

"I'm not dying for this piece of shit, Tammy, and I'm not going to jail either."

"So, what now?"

"I've been thinking. He's the one who did everyone wrong, so why should we all pay. Why should anybody die for his mistakes? I say when he sends us the pictures, we play along with him like we're keeping the plan but instead, we tell Jason and Pop what's going on and set Keys up. They will take care of him and we walk away from everything." I looked at her in amazement.

"They're gonna kill him, Mani. Can you live with that? They might kill us, too!"

"I doubt it, and really, what choice do we have? We can't trust Keys and we don't know what else he's not telling us. They probably killed Mia, Tammy. What if he takes the money and runs, or what if he tries to set us up? I think this is our best way out of this entire situation, what else are can we do?" I went back to staring out the window. My mind was in overdrive. This was Karma kicking me in the ass. If I would've never disrespected Mia and messed with Keys, I wouldn't be in this mess. I didn't like it, but what choice did I have?

"Okay. I'm in, Mani."

"Are you sure?"

"I don't really have a choice, do I?"

"Neither of us do, Tammy. Go home and spend some time with Ty. I'll call you later."

"If you get the text, call me. Okay?" She got out of the car and went in the house.

The whole way home, I couldn't get Mia out of my mind. Keys knew all along who killed her and why. He hugged Mama Walker knowing her daughter was dead because of him.

I can't believe I had sex with him and did the things I did with him. I was disgusted with myself. I wanted to tell Kasey so bad, but I couldn't. Part of me wanted to tell the cops, but I wasn't raised to snitch. Plus, everything would come out and my life would be over. I really felt like Mani's solution was my only option. I just hoped it worked.

In the days that followed, I spent a lot of time at home with Ty. On Friday night, he went out to watch the Miami Heat versus the New York Knicks game with his boys, so Kasey came over to keep me company.

"Girl, what's going on out there? There are police everywhere and an ambulance. They have your whole court blocked off," she said as she came in taking her jacket off.

"I don't know. I was in here cooking with the music on I don't know what happened. Let's go be nosey," I replied. We walked out and saw several of my neighbors outside huddled up talking, so we walked over to see what was going on. A few of them were shaking their heads in disbelief as the paramedics wheeled out the body of my neighbor in a black body bag on a stretcher.

All those times he used to beat her, we all knew about it. I guess none of us thought he would ever take it this far. The police were questioning everyone to see if anyone saw or heard anything and if anyone knew her boyfriend's whereabouts. I text Ty and told him what was going on, so he wouldn't be surprised if he came home and saw all these cops.

Kasey and I went back inside to have a glass of D'usse on the rocks. I took a sip and put the glass down. "Wow, I can't believe he killed her," I said as I took another sip.

"People really are crazy these days."

"Yeah, that's sad. She should've left him. Why let someone put you through that and live life in fear? I don't care how good a man treats you or what he buys you its not worth letting him verbally and physically torment you."

"She did leave a couple of times; she just always came back to him like she couldn't be happy without him. She was never truly happy with him."

We drank and watched videos, laughing, dancing, and goofing off. For a moment, I was lost in laughter and happiness and not focused on death and drama. Then, I got the text from Keys. Suddenly, my whole world stopped. The laughter stopped instantly and my face turned to stone as I looked at the pictures on my phone of the guys he wanted us to set up: Jason and Pop. I couldn't stop staring at my phone. I didn't even hear Kasey talking to me. "Tammy? Hello, earth to Tammy."

I snapped out of it, "Huh? Oh yeah, what's up?"

"You okay? You look like you just saw a ghost."

"Umm yeah, I'm okay. I just have a lot on my mind, but I'm okay. Let's call it a night. I'm tired and I have to get up early, I'll come check you out tomorrow."

"Okay, give me a call after work, so we can go to happy hour or something."

"I sure will. I'll call you when I get home."

I walked Kasey to the door. Then, I called Mani to see if she got the text, and if she was ready for what we were about to do. She told me she got the text, too. She said that she was as ready as she was going to be. I paced around my room mixing and matching different clothes, trying to put together my outfit. My body was here, but my mind was a million miles away. I wondered if Mia was looking down watching everything that was going on. Did she see the mess that my life had become? If she did, I know she was just as disgusted as I was.

⁂

Chapter 8
Carpe Diem

I packed my Gucci duffle bag with my outfit for the night, some accessories, and an extra pair of clothes in case I needed them. I needed to leave before Ty got home, because it was easier for me to lie to him by text or over the phone than face to face. I threw the duffle bag in my trunk and headed over to Mani's. When I got there, she was still in sweat pants and a sweatshirt. She was in the bathroom doing her hair.

I stood in the doorway watching her, "So, we're really about to do this, huh?" I asked. She kept curling her hair and looked at me through the reflection in the mirror. "Yeah Tam, we're going to get this shit over with, move on, and never look back."

"You're so calm and have everything all figured out. I'm over here stressing and driving myself crazy. And what did Keys mean, don't forget how he met you?"

"I figured this would come up one day. Keys met me at a very dark point in my life. I was dancing at Onyx and selling coke for my boyfriend at the time, King. He used to beat the shit out of me whenever he felt like it and treated me like shit. Only reason I stayed was because I had nowhere else to go. We had a nice place. We both had cars and my closet was laced, but with the good comes the bad. The good was great, but the bad was terrible.

He cheated repeatedly and never hesitated to remind me that he could take it all away at the drop of a dime and leave my ass out in the streets. I had the material things I always wanted but I had no privacy or control of my life. He had to know my every move and I had to check in with him if I wasn't home or with him. He made me get rid of all the social media sites that I was on. Went through my phone whenever he felt like it and had to approve of any outfit before I could leave the house in it. He found flaws in all my friends and family and used them to isolate me from them. So I solely depended on him. One day, I came home and he was fucking one of the girls I danced with on our kitchen counter. When I walked in, he didn't even stop. He looked at me, smacked her ass, and kept going. I was so hurt and disgusted, I grabbed my keys and left. Later on that night at Onyx, they were kissing and flirting by the bar and I lost it.

"I started yelling at him about embarrassing and disrespecting me at work. He stood up and smacked me so hard that I fell on the floor under the bar. He threw the bar stool on me and kicked me in the stomach and back until I couldn't breathe. I almost lost consciousness. Everything became blurry. Both the music and voices became muffled, and then the kicking stopped. Keys pulled him off me and fought with him until security broke it up and threw Keys out.

This is how things started with Keys and I. He saved me and I was grateful. I ended up jumping from the frying pan into the fire dealing with Keys. Look where we're at now. I guess this is why I value what we have, because you're the only person in my life right now that see's me for me and treats me with the respect I deserve, even if our situation isn't perfect."

Damn Mani, I had no idea. I'm sorry you went through that. I can't imagine being in that type of situation. I thought I went through shit with Ty. All he did was cheat, which was bad enough, but he was never abusive."

"Tammy, I could sit here for days telling you everything I went through with King, but we don't have the time tonight. Maybe another day I can truly tell you everything," she said as she sat the curling iron down on the bathroom counter and walked into the bedroom.

I stood in the bedroom doorway as she broke down our plan for the night. "So, this is what we're going to do. We go in and get a bottle or two of Rose' and chill for a minute. We play with the strippers for a little while, scoping the crowd for Pop and Jason. When we spot them, we send them a lap dance. After she's done, I'll pull one of them to the side and tell them what's going on."

"Okay, but how do we know they're not going to think we're crazy and blow us off?"

"Would you blow off two hot chicks coming at you with that type of information who know your name and everything? I'm going to show him the text from Keys and everything, Tam, so he believes me and we can all do what we need to do. In the meantime, you entertain his friend."

"Okay, then what?"

"Then, we leave, they walk us out, we get in your car, and follow them to The Loop. While we're on our way there you text Keys and tell him that we're following them and where we're going. When we get there, we'll go inside and get ready for him to come."

"Okay, what's The Loop? And what do we do when he gets there?"

"It's a motel. When he gets there, we let them handle him."

We put our jackets on, grabbed our bags, turned the lights off, and walked out. As we walked to the car and put our bags in the trunk, I looked at Mani. "Let's do this," I said and closed the trunk. The whole ride there I was trying to be normal and act like we had this covered and we were going to be all right, but inside I was a mess. I glanced out the window periodically, feeling lost as my thoughts blended with the music and the blurred scenery as we headed to Jersey Girls. The closer we got, the more nervous I became, but I tried not to let on.

I think Mani could sense it. She was so good at reading me. Before we got out the car, she leaned in and kissed me. I wondered if she was nervous, as well.

"Tammy, text Keys and tell him we're on our way to Jersey Girls, and we'll text him when we're leaving."

"Okay, I have to text Ty. I'm going to tell him we went out to eat and Kasey is meeting us, so he doesn't hit her up."

"Good idea. Make sure you text Kasey, too, so she knows not to go to your house or anything." Kasey wasn't feeling Mani, but because of her loyalty to me, I knew that she would cover for us.

We got to Jersey Girls and followed our plan. It was Sunday, and the place was packed. We made our way around the bar and finally found two seats. I must admit, I always loved strip clubs more than regular clubs because the atmosphere was just better. DJ Envy was in the booth and he was shaking the building with hit after hit. The dancers were showing their skills on the poles and doing tricks on the bars. Hookah was in the air and money was falling from everywhere.

The bartenders were just as sexy as the dancers. I motioned for the one in our section of the bar to come over. We could barely hear each other because the music was so loud, so I put two fingers up and leaned over to get closer to her ear and shouted, "Rose' and hookah!" She nodded and went to tell the runner my order. A few minutes later, she came over with the two bottles in her hand, with sparklers streaming from the tops, and a bucket of ice.

The sparklers on the bottles of liquor or champagne in clubs and strip clubs added affect. They made people look your way and pay attention. It was something that separated you from the average person who was standing around with a cup that couldn't afford bottles or a VIP section. It gave you status in the club. She popped the cork on the Rose' and filled two champagne glasses for us. She sat the bottles in the bucket of ice. We sipped and scanned the room looking for Pop and Jason while we waited for our hookah.

I was also checking out the strippers. I was looking for the baddest one to send over to Jason and Pop when we found them. A beautiful, light-skinned girl with long, shiny curly black hair and ass for days caught my attention and everyone else's. She stretched out completely at the top of the pole. The pole stood seductively between her legs and body.

She grabbed the pole with her hands and bicycle kicked down it for a second and then flipped upside-down. She was working her best acrobatics on the pole while making her plump ass bounce and clap. Money was flying at her from all directions. Then, a cloud of cash came raining down on her all from one direction. When I looked over, I noticed it was Jason. I tapped Mani and looked down at the picture on my phone for confirmation.

She looked at the picture on my phone. Then, she looked at him again and nodded in agreement. That was Jason, but as my eyes searched the room, I didn't see Pop anywhere. I leaned in close to Mani, cupped her ear with my hands, and said, "Where's the other one?" She did the same back to me.

"I don't know. I don't see him." Finally, the hookah guy came over and set our hookah up for us.

I gave him the money and motioned the bartender over again. I gave her five hundred-dollar bills and asked for singles. I took a couple of pulls of hookah and passed it to Mani. When the bartender came back, Mani and I both took about one hundred dollars each in singles and showered the dancer that was drawing all the attention with singles just like Jason had.

As she finished up her routine, I asked the bartender to get her for me. When she hopped off the stage, the bartender sent her our way.

She came over and I gave her one of the stacks of singles and pointed to Jason. "Show him a good time for me," I leaned in and said to her.

"I gotcha, ma'," she replied and winked. Mani and I sipped our Rose' and watched her make her way over to Jason. She leaned in, said something to him, pointed over to Mani and I, and preceded to give him and the bar counter in front of him a very sexy lap dance.

I noticed he had someone else with him, a dark-skinned guy with dreads and a lot of tattoos, but Pop wasn't with him.

"What now?" I leaned in and shouted to Mani.

"I'm gonna go talk to him," she responded as she got up off the chair and made her way over champagne glass in hand. My heart was racing and my throat got dry, so I took another sip of Rose' as my eyes followed her around the bar over to Jason and his friend.

She walked up to him, draped her arm around his neck, and leaned in, so her lips were right by his ear.

"Can I talk to you for a minute?" she asked.

"Thanks for the dance. Do I know you?" he leaned in and replied.

"Not yet, but now that I have your attention, we need to talk. It's important."

"Who said you have my attention?" he sarcastically responded as he stood on the pegs of his barstool and threw another handful of singles at the dancers currently on the stage. I couldn't tell what they were saying from where I was sitting, but the conversation didn't look like it was going in Mani's favor. Then, I saw Mani take her phone out and put it on the counter in front of him.

He looked down at it and looked at her, shocked and confused.

He yelled to his boy, "I'll be right back." Then, he stood up, grabbed Mani by the arm, and walked her outside. I got up and followed them out. He pulled her over to the side of the building and I quickly joined them.

"Who are you and where did you get this picture?"

"I'm Mani and this is Tammy. Keyshawn sent this picture of you and your boy, Pop, to us. He told us you guys would be here and we're supposed to set you up." He took a step back from us and looked around suspiciously like he was waiting for an ambush.

"Who the fuck is Keyshawn? Why did he send y'all instead of coming himself if he's the man?"

"Listen, we're just as clueless as you as to exactly what the problem is," Mani said.

Then, I interjected, "He has some info about us that he's holding over our heads. He promised to forgive and forget if we set you and Pop up. Apparently, someone he does business with has a problem with you guys and wants you out of the picture. We don't want any problems with you and your people. We have a problem with Keys and we want him out the picture, so we figured if we work together, we all win." I wasn't nervous anymore. The liquor must've given me liquid courage or my adrenaline must've kicked in or both. I just wanted this whole situation over with.

"You came here with orders from some punk I don't even know to set up me and my people, and you expect me to believe you and work with you to take him out? Are y'all crazy? I should kill both of you right now."

I looked at him and turned to Mani, "I told you he wouldn't believe us, Mani."

He reached in his pocket and pulled his phone out, Mani and I both jumped. We thought it was a gun. He smirked and called his boy that was inside. "Yo, come meet me outside in the parking lot. We're done for the night." He hung up and put the phone back in his pocket. "Let's take a walk," he said and pointed to the parking lot.

Mani and I looked at each other nervously and followed him. I don't know what was running through her head, but I know what was running through mine. I couldn't believe we were here doing this. How did my life end up like this? Was I going to die tonight and nobody would ever know why? Why did I mess with Keys in the first place? Those passionate encounters weren't worth what we were now caught up in. I grabbed Mani's hand as he walked us to his car where his friend was waiting. He pressed the remote to the pearl white Porsche Panamera and told us to get in.

I let go of her hand, opened the back-left passenger door, and got in. She walked around the car, opened the back-right passenger door, and got in. Jason got in the driver's side and his friend got in the front passenger seat.

He looked at his friend. "So, apparently we have a situation. Ladies introduce yourselves to my boy."

I looked at Mani and hesitated, waiting for her to speak first. "I'm Mani and this is Tammy."

Then Jason spoke, "Mani and Tammy were sent by some punk ass fool named Keys to set us up."

His boy turned around and looked at us. "Oh yeah. Keys sent y'all to get at us? You got the heart to do it?" he asked.

Jason answered for us, "Nah. Instead, they want us to do him." They both started laughing, and I got a bad feeling that their laughter might mean our pain.

I gave Tammy the what now look, and she gave it right back to me. Then, Jason started the car and adjusted the rearview mirror, so he could see us and we could see him. "Buckle up, ladies. We're gonna take a little ride," he said with a smirk as he sped out of the parking lot. I got the feeling our plan was out the window. They now had plans of their own for us. My thoughts were scattered as I tried to figure a way out for Mani and I.

I felt like a ball of nerves. I was nauseous and scared, but I had to figure out something and quick. As he drove, his boy whose name we still didn't know sparked a Newport, cracked the window, and turned the music up. The night air blowing on us in the back helped a little with my nausea, but not much. I slid my phone out my back pocket and held it down between my left calf and the door so they couldn't see me texting. Ty kept calling and texting me wondering where I was. So I text him back that I was with Mani and she had too much to drink and got sick. I told him I was going to take her home and get her settled, and then I would be home right after. Mani nervously watched, hoping I wouldn't get caught. I turned the location feature off on my phone, so he couldn't tell where we were. Then, I slid the phone back into my pocket. Mani looked at me and motioned with her lips, Who? I motioned back, Ty. Her whole facial expression changed.

We rode for what seemed like forever, inhaling second-hand smoke from his friend who by now was three Newports in. We were listening to him argue on the phone with whom I would guess was his girlfriend about what time it is and why he still wasn't home. I guess it was starting to annoy Jason, too, because he turned the music down and told him, "Man, handle that shit later. We got business to tend to and you're on the phone arguing like a little bitch. And no more cigs. You got my fucking car stinking."

He opened the sunroof and turned the music back up. His friend hung up the phone, and we went back to riding in silence. I looked out the window trying to figure out where we were. All I knew from the signs I saw, was we were somewhere in Hillside, but I had no idea where. I wasn't familiar with the area at all. We had made so many twists and turns that I was completely lost.

Chapter 9
The Beginning of the End

My phone vibrated in my back pocket. Just as I went to slide it out my pocket and text like before, the car slowed down and we pulled into a driveway. Mani and I looked at each other with terror in our eyes as Jason put the car in park, opened the door, and got out. His boy followed his lead. Jason tossed the keys to his boy and told him to go through the house and open the garage door. The garage door opened, his boy tossed the keys back to him, and Jason got back in the car. He drove the car into the garage and his boy closed the door and locked it.

Jason got out the car first and opened the back door for me.

"Get out," he demanded, standing by the door with a stern look on his face. I stubbornly sat there for a minute trying to buy time. Mani stared at me with a scared and lost look in her eyes.

"I'm not going to tell you again, get out, both of you." As he demanded again, his boy opened Mani's door and gave her the same look Jason was giving me.

As we got out, nausea swept over me and I threw up on the garage floor. Jason jumped back, so the vomit wouldn't splash off the garage floor onto him. His boy shook his head, looked at Mani, and said, "That ain't sexy." He closed the car door and walked over to a chair in the corner and had a seat. I finished throwing up and Jason went in his trunk got a towel out and tossed it to me, "Clean yourself up, and both of you get over here." Mani and I walked around the front of the car waiting for whatever it was he was going to do to us. He looked at us and extended his hand. "Give me your phones," he demanded.

Then, Jason looked over at his boy. "Go get the guns," he ordered. His boy walked through the door that connected the garage to the house, and Mani and I handed our phones to him. I don't know which was racing faster my heart or my thoughts.

Mani started pleading for our lives, "You don't have to do this. I promise we won't tell anybody anything just let us go. We're sorry. We don't want to die and we didn't want you to die either. That's why we came to you."

Jason cut Mani off. "Shhh," he whispered as he put his index finger to his lips.

His boy walked back in the garage with two black handguns, one in each hand as Jason pushed two chairs together and pointed at them. "Have a seat," he said.

My palms were sweating and my stomach was twisting and turning like I was on a Six Flags rollercoaster. As I forced myself to sit down in the chair, all I could think of was how much I didn't want to die. He walked over to Mani and handed her the phone.

"This is how it's going down. Text your boy, Keys, and tell him change of plans. Tell him y'all are on your way back to my place with me and Pop, and you're gonna turn on the GPS on your phone, so he can find us."

Mani did as Jason said. She text Keys and turned the GPS on.

We waited for Keys' response while Jason filled us in on the rest of his plan.

"We're gonna wait for your boy to get here. When he does, y'all are gonna take him out. Either one of y'all ever shot a gun before?" he asked.

Mani and I both responded simultaneously, "No."

"Well, there's a first time for everything."

As he was laying out his plan, Keys text back that he was on his way with his boy. Jason instructed Mani, "Text him back and tell him it's the house with the white Porsche Panamera parked in front. Pull up in front of the Porsche, turn the lights off, and text Mani when he's outside." She did as he said.

Jason's boy stood watching us, holding both guns with one visibly tucked in the front of his jeans as Jason went over his plans with us. As he slowly paced back and forth with my phone in his hand, it vibrated, interrupting him. He looked down at a picture of Ty on my phone with the Caller ID name Babe and looked up at me.

"Who the fuck is this, your man?" he asked.

My heart dropped and Mani gave me the, *oh shit,* look again as I responded. "Yes, but he has nothing to do with this. He doesn't even know that either of us deal with Keys."

He hit ignore on the phone. "How do I know he's not in on this with y'all and Keys?" he asked.

"Let me call him back. I'll talk to him right in front of you. Please don't drag him into this. He's one of the reasons I agreed to do this. Keys has pictures and info that could destroy us."

"This Keys guy sounds like a real class A dude. I guess he has some mean shit on you too, huh ma?" He laughed and looked at Mani.

He tossed the phone to me, "Call him now."

I nervously called Ty back, scrambling to get my thoughts together, so he could understand me without tipping off Jason.

The phone rang once and Ty answered, "Tammy, where are you. Are you okay? You didn't text me back."

I tried not to let him hear the fear in my voice, "Hey babe. I'm okay. I'm with Mani. Listen, my phone keeps losing service. I'll call you back when we get settled, okay?" I said and quickly hung up.

I handed the phone back to Jason. "See, I told you he doesn't know anything. He's just looking for me because it's late and I'm not home yet." Then, Mani's phone went off. It was Keys texting back.

Jason looked down at the phone and read the text and looked up at us, "He'll be here in twenty minutes. Let's get this shit together. Text him back and tell him that you're going to tell me that Tammy left her phone in the car and you're going to go outside and get it. When you come out, him and his boy are gonna follow you back in and take us out. Tell him we're drunk in the living room chilling with Tammy. All they have to do is sneak in the living room and handle their business."

Mani text everything to Keys the way Jason told her. She then gave him the phone back and asked, "Now what?"

"Now, you two listen very closely and do as I say, exactly as I say, and you get to live. Get any bright ideas or try anything stupid, and you're gonna die with your friend. When he gets here, you go outside just like you text him. Walk them up to the side door. As soon as you get to the side door, my boy is gonna come from behind you and put the heat to them. At the same time, me and my little cousin that's in the house right now waiting by the door are going to open the door and bring them in.

This is where you come in. Mani, since you seem like the stronger one out of the two of y'all, you get to do the honors. We're gonna knock them out, take their guns, and bring them in the garage. Mani, you're gonna shoot Keys. I'm gonna shoot his boy, and just to make sure you don't try anything while you have the gun, Tammy's gonna stay tied up in here and my little cousin will keep the gun on her until it's over. You get any bright ideas, she's dead and so are you." Mani and I looked at him horrified as he took one of the guns from his boy and instructed him to tie me up.

His boy tied me to the chair while he called his cousin and told him to come to the garage.

"Get up, Mani. Come here. Before I hand the gun to you, I'm going to take the safety off. Point it at his head, aim, and squeeze. It's a hair trigger, so it's gonna fire easy. If you freeze up or try any funny shit, your girl dies and so do you. Trust me, my cousin won't hesitate to blow her pretty little brains out. Everything goes right, we take you back to your car, you go home, and forget you ever met us."

His cousin walked in the garage. Jason pointed to me.

"They should be here any minute. After we bring them in here, you hold the gun on her. If anything goes wrong, blow her fucking head off."

His cousin looked at me, looked at Jason, and nodded in agreement.

"Go back by the door and wait for me," Jason ordered.

His boy finished tying me up, and then went outside and hid on the side of the porch. I could tell Mani was scared to death, but at this point, I think we both realized it was kill or be killed. Neither of us was ready to die.

As I sat there tied to the chair all I could think about was Ty. I had no idea where he was or what he was doing. All I could do is pray. I prayed harder than I've ever prayed before, hoping God would get us out of this alive. I was promised God and myself that I'd never cheat again and I'd live right if he just got us out of here alive. I couldn't believe I was sitting here tied to a chair in a garage about to watch Mani and a man I just met three hours ago kill Keys.

I kept wishing it was all a bad dream and I was gonna wake up home in my bed with Ty, but I knew it wasn't. Then, Mani's phone went off. It was Keys. They were outside parked in front of the Porsche with the lights off.

Jason walked Mani to the door, "Stick to the plan, Mani, and this will all be over soon. Remember, no slick shit or your girl gets it. Walk him to the door nice and slow." I sat in the garage by myself tied to the chair, scared to death, fighting back tears, and unable to see or hear anything that was going on.

Mani knew everything depended on her as she nervously walked out to the Porsche and hit the button on the keypad to disarm the alarm and unlock the doors. Keys and his boy got out of Keys' car and ducked down by Jason's car. They both pulled their guns out and took the safety's off.

"You ready?" Keys whispered to Mani.

"Shhh," she answered, putting her finger up to her lip and ducking down behind the car.

"Where are they?" Keys whispered.

"In the living room. Be quiet and follow me. When we get in, walk right behind me. When I turn left, y'all turn right, and they'll be right there. Tammy knows what to do when she sees me walk back in, so she's out of the way. Now come on, before they start looking for me."

The driveway was pitch black. The only light to guide Mani back to the side porch was the moonlight and the faint glow of a streetlight across the street and one house over.

She got to the porch and slowly walked up the stairs. As she turned the doorknob, Jason's boy popped up off the side of the porch and hit Keys boy in the head with the gun. He fell to the ground and his gun flew out of his hand into the grass. At the same time, the door flew open. Mani dropped to her knees on the ground as Jason and his cousin put their guns to Keys head.

"Give me that shit," Jason's cousin said as he snatched the gun from Keys. Mani crawled between him and the small space in the door way and ran into the garage. Jason's boy kicked and stomped Keys boy until he passed out. Jason and his cousin walked Keys into the garage at gunpoint. Mani ran over to me and stood behind me. Jason's boy dragged Keys' boy in the garage while Jason gave out orders.

"Mani, get over here," he said while keeping the gun on Keys. Then, he told his cousin, "Give Mani some motivation to handle her business."

His cousin walked over and put his gun to my head. At that moment, I was sure I was going to die. Tears started streaming uncontrollably down my face as I awaited my fate.

Jason looked Keys in his eyes and smiled, "See what happens when you send a girl to do a man's job?"

Keys stared at him for a second, looked to the left at me, and then to the right at Mani.

"Do you think this shit is going to end with me? My peoples are gonna come for you. Believe that," Keys said to Jason.

"Are those your last words? Now it's my turn. They'll be too busy looking for your body," Jason replied. Then, he pulled the trigger.

Blood and brain matter splattered onto Jason, Mani, and the floor as Keys limp body fell to the ground. I sat speechless, stunned, and in shock. I'd never seen anyone die before. It happened so quick I didn't even have time to look away or brace myself. Mani froze and stood there with blood on her. She began shaking. Jason walked over to Keys and shot him again in the head. Then, he grabbed Mani's arm and pulled her over to where his boy was standing over Keys' boy with the gun pointed at him. "Give her your gun," he said to his boy as he held his gun pressed against her head.

Mani wrapped her fingers around the gun, gripping the rubber handle and shaking so bad she could hardly hold it. My stream of tears turned into a river as I feared I would watch her die next. Keys' boy sat on the garage floor beaten, bleeding, and half-conscious as Jason pressed his gun against Mani's head.

"Do it or y'all both die, too." Tears rolled down Mani's face as she fought with her emotions.

"Do it!" he screamed. Mani gripped the gun with both hands, aimed it at his head, and pulled the trigger.

⁇

Chapter 10
It Ain't Over 'til It's Over

Mani dropped the gun and collapsed to the floor, still in shock. Keys' boy's lifeless body lay on the floor in front of her as thick, dark blood formed a puddle around his head. I sat glued to the chair in shock, too. I couldn't believe she actually shot and killed a man in front of me. This is what it had come to. Our lives were out of control. Jason picked up the gun with the sleeve of his shirt and walked around to the trunk of his car. He popped the trunk and dropped the gun in a brown and beige Louis Vuitton bag in his trunk. Then, he grabbed a dark gray Champion hoodie out the trunk and closed it.

He ordered his cousin to untie me. Then, he walked over to Mani, grabbed her by the arm, and stood her up. He looked her in the eyes. "Shake that shit off, ma."

Then, he told his boy to take her to the bathroom, so she could clean up and he tossed the hoodie to Mani. She was so caught up in her emotions that she didn't even reach out to catch it. It bounced off her onto the floor and Jason picked it up.

"Yo, I said snap the fuck out of it already," he yelled at Mani and tossed the hoodie at her.

This time, she put her hands out and caught it. I exhaled with a small sigh of relief. I felt the atmosphere getting tense. The last thing I wanted was for her to set him off. He pushed Mani toward his boy who walked her in the house to the bathroom.

"Hurry up. We ain't got all day," he said to Mani as she walked in the bathroom and shut the door.

She stared at herself in the mirror for a minute trying to find herself in the reflection. As she looked down at the blood on her shirt, visions of Keys danced around in her head like she was flipping through pages in a mental photo album.

She saw them eating at Houllihan's, riding around in his car laughing, and listening to music. Him dancing in her bedroom doorway in his boxer briefs, goofing around after sex, and him kissing her on the cheek, and putting her in his car the night he saved her from King.

Her heart got heavy and her emotions overpowered her as she put her face in her hands and broke down in tears. She couldn't believe what she'd done and felt worse and worse by the minute. Jason's boy was banging on the door telling Mani to come out, but she wouldn't respond. Jason's cousin untied me and Jason told me to get in the car and wait for him. I walked around the perimeter of the garage, because I didn't want to come close to Keys' body. I couldn't even look at him. The smell of their blood in the garage was making me nauseous. I prayed they would hurry up before I threw up again. Jason got tired of waiting and went to see what was taking Mani and his boy so long. When he got to the bathroom, his boy was pounding on the door and Mani wouldn't come out. Jason pushed him to the side and banged on the door.

"Come out or I'm gonna kick it in!"

Mani jumped and replied, "Okay, okay, give me a second." She washed her face and hands, threw the hoodie he gave her on over her shirt, and then opened the door.

"Let's go," Jason demanded as he led the way back to the garage. Mani walked over to the car and got in. As Jason walked to the car, he told his cousin and his boy to start cleaning up the mess and that he was taking us to our car.

Mani and I sat still as statues in the backseat as Jason drove to Jersey Girls. I glanced at Mani a couple of times trying to get her attention, but she never looked anywhere but straight from the moment she got in the car. We drove for a few minutes in silence again. Then, all of a sudden, Mani jumped on Jason, punching him and fighting him. He yelled and swerved, trying to fight her off and regain control the car. Cars were coming and he was losing control. I felt the car fishtailing and I jumped on both of them trying to get between them and grab the wheel, but it was too late.

The left side of the car smashed into the guard rail and bounced off the rail into the car to the right of us. Both cars were going so fast that after we collided, we bounced off of the car and flipped over the guard rail. The last thing I saw was the world upside down as the car flipped over the guard rail and landed upside down on its roof on the opposite side of the highway. Everything went black and I heard a horn beeping loudly then felt a hard smack of impact and passed out as we were hit by an SUV going too fast to stop.

Police, EMTs, and firefighters arrived promptly to the scene as motorists watched horrified. Jason was pronounced dead at the scene. Mani and I were air lifted to the nearest trauma center which was Jersey Shore Medical Center. They rushed us both in for surgery. I had two huge gashes in my head, and my brain was swelling from the impact. I also suffered a broken femur, three broken ribs, and lacerations on my hand. I made it out of surgery, but was in a coma.

Mani wasn't so lucky. Her pelvis was crushed; she had broken ribs and a lot of internal bleeding as well as two breaks in her tibia and severe head trauma. They tried to save her, but there was just too much internal bleeding. She didn't make it. After eight days, I opened my eyes. I was intubated and in a lot of pain, but I was alive. Ty and my mom were right there by my side. They went crazy when I opened my eyes, calling the nurses, holding my hand, kissing me, and thanking God.

In the days that followed, I was in and out of consciousness, but they filled me in on everything that had happened since the accident and everything they were told. They told me how Mani and the other guy in the car, Jason, both didn't make it. They also told me how I was in a coma and had missed their funerals. Ty told me he went to Mani's services and paid his respects on behalf of both of us and got me an obituary to read when I get home. The cops found a gun in the bag in Jason's car and wanted to know, if or when I woke up, if I knew who it belonged to. As I faded in and out for days, processing the information they were spoon feeding me, I randomly got flashes of Keys lying dead with blood slowly streaming from his body.

Then, it hit me. The images were real. Even with the head trauma, I remembered flashes of what happened. Keys was dead, but nobody was saying anything about that. The visions were blurry and my head wasn't right, so I couldn't quite figure everything out, but I had a feeling that in a matter of time, it would all come back. The question is, will I be ready when it does? Right now everyone is just happy and grateful that I miraculously survived.

But, I know in due time my family and the police will have a lot of questions that only I have the answers to. When they do, they'll get what I conveniently remember. It's crazy how love changes lives, how lines get crossed when there are feelings involved, and how there's a story behind every story.

About the Author

Born in Philadelphia raised in New Jersey, Tuanika learned early that discipline and determination are the key elements to success. Raised in a single parent home with no father, she learned from her mother and the streets how to survive and succeed. After losing the father of her unborn child at the age of 18 to a fiery car accident, she too became a single parent. With the weight of the world on her shoulders and a daughter to provide for, she quickly figured out that a minimum wage job wasn't going to be enough and turned to the streets. Coming from a family that ranged from kingpin drug dealers to jazz musicians and famous artists, she was a blend of both worlds. Selling drugs and working supported her, all while using writing as an outlet.

In the years that followed, the deaths of family members and many friends fueled her fire to get out of the streets and provide a better life for her and her children. Inspired by the passion and success of her uncle who is well known artist Calvin Massey, she turned her focus to writing and received an Omega Psi Phi award for her literary work. Tuanika then began her journey to become a known author and started working on her first novel. Halfway through, she was involved in a horrific car accident that nearly ended her life. While recovering, she refused to let her setbacks deter her from her dreams of becoming a published author. Through hard work and determination, she turned her dream into a reality and completed her first novella *Subliminal*.